From Baby To Babe Magnet!

By Nick Hansen, columnist,
Pittsburgh Register

It is a truth universally acknowledged that no woman can resist a baby. Thinking about that, it occurred to me that there is an absolutely surefire combination that will attract even the most resistant unattached woman out there—a single dad with a toddler in tow. So, in the name of research (honest!), I decided to put my hunch to the test. And, reader, please don't hate me, but, yes, I borrowed a baby to prove my point....

Dear Reader,

There's just something irresistible about a big strong guy holding a little tiny baby, or maybe bouncing a chubby-cheeked toddler on his knee. In fact, I'm surprised more guys haven't figured out that the perfect way to attract a woman is by accessorizing themselves in just that way. Nick Hansen's got it figured out, though. The hero of Leslie Davis Guccione's *Borrowed Baby* has decided that fake fatherhood—and his resulting romantic successes—will make a perfect subject for his newspaper column. He just hasn't figured out quite what to do about irresistible Shannon McEvoy—or the fact that he's falling in love with a woman with one very big misconception about him!

Then check out *Fiancé for the Night,* by newcomer Melissa McClone. There's nothing like a sham engagement to start the sparks flying. The problem Cassandra Daniels is having with that, though, is that she's finding herself much more attracted to Troy McKnight, her bogus bridegroom-to-be, than she planned. Now she's wondering whether there's any chance of those sparks lighting the kind of fire that's meant to last a lifetime.

Yours,

Leslie Wainger
Executive Senior Editor

Please address questions and book requests to:
Silhouette Reader Service
U.S.: 3010 Walden Ave., P.O. Box 1325, Buffalo, NY 14269
Canadian: P.O. Box 609, Fort Erie, Ont. L2A 5X3

LESLIE DAVIS GUCCIONE

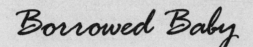

Borrowed Baby

Published by Silhouette Books

America's Publisher of Contemporary Romance

For Amy and Meg, my sudden summer visitors,

and

The rowers and writers of Pittsburgh who shared
four wonderful years,
especially fellow author Karen Lynn Williams

 SILHOUETTE BOOKS

ISBN 0-373-52089-1

BORROWED BABY

Copyright © 1999 by Leslie Davis Guccione

Dear Reader,

In the midst of starting my writing career in Boston, I fell in love with a guy complete with toddler in tow. Twenty-five years later, as a family of five, we're still living happily ever after, and twenty-five years into my career, I'm still convinced it's a great premise for someone else's love story. It just needed a few twists.

What if our hero, handsome, self-assured, successful columnist Nick Hansen, thinks there's nothing more irresistible to single women than an eligible single father, and intends to bolster his journalistic reputation by writing a magazine article on how he proved it? What if our confident hero has to borrow a child to illustrate his point; conceal his identity to conduct the project; lacks the parental skills to keep the little guy happy; and runs smack into the attractive, creative—suspicious—woman of his dreams…who despises every word he's written?

I hope you'll have as much pleasure following the exploits of Shannon McEvoy and Nick Hansen as I did creating them. Mine may be a match made in heaven. This one's a match made over geraniums and crumpled newsprint.

Watch for the secondary love story in this one, too— my tribute to the great city of Pittsburgh, its rivers, its rowers, its writers. With the possible exception of Boston, there's no better place to fall in love.

Happy reading!

Leslie Davis Guccione

Books by Leslie Davis Guccione

Silhouette Yours Truly

Borrowed Baby

Silhouette Desire

Before the Wind #279
*Bittersweet Harvest #311
*Still Waters #353
*Something in Common #376
*Branigan's Touch #523
*Private Practice #554
A Gallant Gentleman #674
Rough and Ready #713
A Rock and a Hard Place #748
Derek #795
Major Distractions #870
*Branigan's Break #902

* Branigan Brothers series

1

Remember, men, she may tell you it's roses and candlelight she wants, but it's your TV remote she's really after.

Nicholas Hansen searched for the usual sense of satisfaction as he tapped out the last sentence of his newspaper column:

Relinquish it at your peril.

"The rewards of self-discipline," he muttered while he ran the copy through the spell check. Once it was saved and set to be printed, he stretched his jean-clad legs and swiveled in his desk chair to the window in time to catch sight of a tugboat as it eased its coal barges down the last stretch of the Allegheny River. The afternoon sun glinted off Pittsburgh's spectacular skyline.

The Allegheny and Monongahela met to form the Ohio River along the desirable waterfront property that included Three Rivers Stadium, Roberto Clemente Park and the fountains of the Point. The stunning cityscape filled the steep terrain that formed cliffs and bluffs straight down to the water's edges. Nick ran his hand through his wheat-colored hair and arched his complaining back muscles. He'd earned this view. Never mind that it included the riverfront editorial offices of both the *Pittsburgh Register* and *Three Rivers Magazine.* His editor, Dan Miller, was at the paper impatiently waiting for this afternoon's promised copy, copy it was tougher and tougher to keep fresh. Fifteen minutes earlier Nick had assured Charlie Hutchinson at the magazine that he'd make their deadline as well. Okay, so he'd put off the assignment till the last minute.

Nick raised his coffee mug in salute. He'd been on the river at dawn, sculling in his one-man shell well before the rising wind or commercial traffic kicked up the current, about the time his weekly column in the *Register* was being tossed against stoops and onto front porches from Point Breeze to Polish Hill.

His morning routine was head-clearing, endorphin-surging time, meant to keep his mental valves clean and the pumps working. Ten years out of the University of Pittsburgh's journalism program and he could still hear his college crew coach every time he pulled on the oars.

While the printer hummed he looked at the ever-present stack of mail, most addressed to Jake O'Donnell in care of the *Register.* He toasted his cigar-chomping, whiskey-toting mentor. "To you, Jake. God bless your sardonic soul." Nick Hansen had been the anonymous voice behind "Jake O'Donnell: Since You Asked" since the hard driving, hard drinking, sixty-eight-year-old had dropped dead during a Penguins game four years ago.

Nick took over the column without fanfare. At thirty-one Nick Hansen's fresh, acerbic view of the battle of the sexes had parlayed the local column into syndication and journalistic tributes, but it was still Jake O'Donnell's byline and Jake's head shot on the column. It had been Nick's idea to move the column from the masculine pages of the sports section to the Living pages, which tended to focus on house tours, book reviews and the arts. Beyond that, he'd had a semiannual argument with his editor over any kind of update.

"*Nick Hansen.* It's got the same no-nonsense ring as *Jake O'Donnell* and your publicity shot's a damn sight easier on the eyes than Jake's bulldog-ugly puss. The amount of fan mail you generate is a sure indication that we can make the change with no repercussions," Dan was always telling him.

Sure as the Steelers were perennial Superbowl material, repercussions would be in his personal life, not at the editorial desk. "There's a certain number of letters I wouldn't categorize as fan mail," Nick always replied. No sir. Jake O'Donnell's name and grizzled granite face on the head shot suited Nick just fine. It gave him the anonymity he wanted in his life and for the moment it was absolutely necessary if he were to pull off his next assignment with ease.

The phone rang and jolted him out of his reverie

as he met his sister's greeting with a yawn and an apology. "Sorry, Kate. Long day and it's not over yet." He drained the mug.

"I'll bet that's cold coffee on an empty stomach," Kate Hansen Goulding replied. "Listen, big brother, I'm sure I'm not the first to point out that there are saner ways to make a deadline than getting up at dawn and overloading on adrenaline and caffeine for the rest of the day."

"Don't you have some packing to do?"

"Finished. I called to remind you to be prompt tonight so you can spend some time with Nicholas before he goes to bed. You know what a handful he is at bath time. I want to make sure you can handle it. Give Paul and me one less thing to worry about while we're at the cottage. Are you going to be on time?"

"Absolutely. I need time to work on his nickname."

"Nick, I know you like calling him Kip, but he'll have enough confusion this week."

"Two Nicholases is enough confusion." He changed the subject. "Hear that humming printer? Three weeks worth of columns are rolling out right now. As soon as I fax them to the desk, there's nothing on my agenda but my nephew and my brilliant sociological study."

"I have to admire your guts," Kate replied. "There are enough women loose on the streets of Pittsburgh already who'd like to hang you out to dry."

"Proof that they're reading every word they complain about. Besides, my project's nothing more than observation and comment on established feminine behavior.''

Kate laughed. ''Call it what you like. You're using my two-year-old to pick up women and then report the gory details in *Three Rivers Magazine*. Watch your backside, Nick.''

Nick laughed. ''Don't give either of us another thought. I've been part of Kip's life since his first days. You've drilled me in every fine point on parenthood imaginable and have let me practice most of it. We'll do just fine. Besides, High Pines is less than an hour's drive away. If I fail, I'll deliver him myself and admit defeat.''

''It's not your parenting skills that worry me. Paul and I don't want to drive in from High Pines to post your bail or replace your scalp when the female population of Pittsburgh discovers that you're trying to prove it's easier to pick up women when they think you're a single father. Your toddler-in-tow scheme could only have been hatched in a haze of cigar smoke and beer foam in the back room of some East Carson Street bar.''

''Please. I got the original idea from a fellow journalist, female, if you must know. It's a sociological study Charlie Hutchinson begged for.'' Nick ignored her snicker. Last fall during a nailbiter of a Steelers game the features editor of *Three Rivers Magazine* had begun his annual pitch to get him to pose for the summer issue on Pittsburgh's most eligible singles and Nick had begun his annual refusal. No way was he going to blow his cover and have his name and face connected with the Jake O'Donnell column. To placate Charlie he'd suggested the idea of the article instead—as long as he could write it under his real name. Anything to get the editor to stop insisting and focus on the action. Dan had been with them and later over a round—or two—in an East Carson Street bistro, even he had assured Hutchinson that the paper would lend Nick out since he was the perfect journalist to put a spin on observed female behavior.

This was no seat-of-your-pants assignment. He was moving into his sister's town house and borrowing the toddler to transform himself for a week's worth of intense study. To further simplify the relationship he would no longer be Nicholas Hansen, adored uncle. He was about to become Nicholas Goulding, young Nicholas Goulding's bachelor father. Nick and Kip going off to meet admiring women: He liked his concept already. This assignment would be a lot less demanding than composing the syndicated columns he slaved over. Hell, this assignment was going to be fun.

He picked up his work from the copier. "Gotta run, Kate. These columns need proofreading and I need the phone to fax them to the office. Tell Kip I'll be there at six."

"Nick, you won't forget that he takes constant watching? While Paul and I are gone there's to be no more staring at that computer screen for hours. No more writing, faxing—"

He caught the hesitation in his sister's voice. "Pencil and journal until he's asleep, just as I promised. Laptop after he's in bed. I have to write, Kate, I have a mighty tight deadline.''

''You've had all winter.''

''You know how I work.'' He paused. ''Are you having second thoughts about my parenting skills?''

She sighed. ''Remind me that if I didn't think you were capable, I wouldn't be doing this.''

''You know I love that little guy like he was my own. Clean clothes, proper diet, strict schedule, lots of sleep,'' Nick replied.

''That goes for my son, too,'' she offered back.

''Cute, Kate. We'll go over it all tonight. Thurston Court at six o'clock. You can lecture me then.''

With Kate off the phone he proofread and faxed his required columns to the *Register.* ''Done,'' he said out loud as he took his empty coffee mug off the mouse pad and the T-shirt from the stack of framed diplomas, award-winning articles and tributes for his volunteer efforts on behalf of Pittsburgh's inner city rowing program. One of these days he'd get around to hanging them on his still-blank wall. Laundry was next.

He needed a week's worth of clothes and he was down to cast-offs and button-down collars. He plucked his sweatshirt off the bookcase where it draped over a collegiate rowing trophy, but even with the clothing in his arms, it did little to alleviate the clutter of the third floor combination of loft and home office.

Nick yawned downstairs again as he packed his

washing machine. Kate was right. He loved kick-starting his day with a sunrise workout at the boat-house and a six-mile row. In college the routine had flooded him with enough endorphins to see him through any assignment, but at thirty-one he now aug-mented adrenaline with a steady flow of caffeine, too often on an empty stomach. He pressed the acid-induced gnaw at his belt. One of his sister's home cooked dinners was a sure cure.

In the meantime he pulled the familiar white boxes embossed with Chinese characters from the refriger-ator and stuck the remains of last night's takeout in the microwave oven. The Jade Dragon was a favorite haunt and the leftovers would tide him over till he got to Thurston Court.

With the assignment complete, fatigue seeped its way between his shoulder blades. While the washing machine churned, he settled down with fried rice, the ever-present stack of mail and a cold beer on the deck off the living room. On the river, powerboats had re-placed the barge and a few were still puttering around the marina just beyond the town houses. The nearly perfect June day was sliding into late afternoon. Nick propped his feet on the railing. The Pirates were in town and fireworks were scheduled over the stadium after the double-header. Maybe he could hustle Kip out of bed to watch the light show. Pittsburgh prided itself on its fireworks. Nick sipped his beer and grinned. It was a line he'd used more than once when referring to the explosive nature of so many of his columns.

* * *

The following afternoon Shannon McEvoy knelt on her brick walk and laid out the crumpled newspaper she needed to catch the soil as she repotted her flats of geraniums. "Jake O'Donnell: Since You Asked" smoothed out under the heel of her hand. "I didn't ask," she muttered as she glanced at the month-old column.

Male bonding. What feminist support group dreamed up that oxymoron? A generation ago male bonding was a fellow in his basement with pipe clamps and wood glue. Sharing my Sky Box Civic Arena seats aren't enough? Now I'm supposed to bear my soul to the guy I took to the play-offs. I'll save the heartfelt hugs for the gender less laden with testosterone, someone unlikely to start the day pulling a razor over a lathered jaw.

She shook her head and knocked the first pot of soil over the rest of the column. That week's testosterone-laden "Since You Asked" shared the Living section of the *Register* with a photo essay on laying out a knot-shaped herb garden, recipes for the last of spring's fresh spinach and directions for marbleizing bathroom walls. Some editor's way to generate publicity for O'Donnell through female indignation, no doubt. Mentally she'd penned a few outraged responses herself but anonymous letters were cowardly and she wasn't about to use a return address that might languish in Jake O'Donnell's file drawer.

Besides, with her move to the Pittsburgh town house, her business brisk in Time Out, her Walnut Street children's shop, and her volunteer efforts at Children's Hospital, she barely had time to read the paper, let alone to write a letter to it. She still had mounds of unpacking and arranging to do but despite the fact that it had only been forty-eight hours, Thurston Court was beginning to feel like home.

She'd killed the morning at the shop, opening it for a photo shoot for *Three Rivers Magazine.* A month ago freelance journalist Karen Holland had proposed a profile piece on her as a single entrepreneurial woman. It seemed ironic that the feature on her and her shop would run in the Pittsburgh's Most Eligible Singles issue when she catered primarily to young mothers. Still, it was publicity for her business and she needed all she could get.

She also needed the fresh air filling her lungs. The McEvoy brothers will approve, she thought affectionately as she worked her spade into the dirt and blew at her coppery bangs. She wiped her forehead with the back of her dirty cuff. Evan, the youngest of her three older half brothers, was to be her first guest. She'd invited him to dinner, provided he brought it with him.

She grouped the geraniums tenderly by color on the newspaper and admired the early blooms. The corals and pinks would be spectacular in another few weeks. She peeled off her gardening gloves and considered a border of lamb's ears or dusty miller for its silvery foliage. She hadn't scrimped on soil preparation any more than on the hybrid geraniums. Whatever she chose would thrive.

The heat of the day was arriving and Shannon pulled the band from her tangled hair. She stepped backward on the sidewalk to consider the geraniums' placement and rewind her topknot, up away from her neck and the scoop-neck shirt already smudged with compost. As she worked her hair back up, something landed against the back of her knees. She stumbled and nearly lost her balance as she tried to turn around. An overall-clad toddler was tangled in her legs.

"Goodness, where did you come from?" she cried. He rocked on his tiny sneakers and landed squarely on his well-padded bottom. Shannon continued to apologize as she knelt, but at five feet ten inches, she still towered over him. He looked up at her with dark, wide eyes the color of chestnuts. His thatch of blond hair framed a face that began to crumple. His lower lip went first.

"Don't cry, sweetie," she murmured. Shannon dusted off her hands and helped him up by his overall straps, afraid if she pulled him into her arms she'd loosen the floodgates, already threatening to overflow.

"Mommy—"

"We'll find her." She offered her hand and looked bleakly down the lane. Her house was just three doors in from the brick-walled entrance that separated the sedate complex from the bustle of Pittsburgh's Fifth Avenue. Thurston Court encompassed fifty town houses along a horseshoe-curved street and a patchwork of cul-de-sacs. Mommy could be anywhere.

Well down the block two teenage girls sat on a front porch. An elderly man knelt in his own garden across the way. "I don't suppose you belong to any of those," she inquired.

"Mommy—"

"I know. I know. Did you come from a backyard? How about from around the bend?"

"Mommy" grew tremulous.

Shannon knelt again. He backed up. "What's your name, sweetheart?"

"Nick."

At least it sounded like *Nick*. "*Nick?*" Shannon stood.

"Kip." His lip stopped quivering. "Nick."

"Kipnick? Okay, that's a start. Do you have a first name little Kipnick?"

"Mommy—"

Maybe he was saying *Tommy*. "*Tommy Kipnick?*" He shook his head and tears pooled in his thick lashes. His hand tightened around her fingers. Shannon tried to think logically. She'd been gardening for nearly an hour. She'd sat on her stoop and rested at the curb. Surely if he were a neighbor, she'd have seen him playing or spotted him with a parent or sitter, unless he'd just escaped from inside an unsuspecting household.

Someone was damned irresponsible. "Did you just sneak out of your house? Can you show me?"

He hiccuped and took a hesitant step forward, not toward the row houses, but in the direction of the bustling avenue beyond the walled entrance. Tears spilled.

"Don't cry," she murmured but her heart fell. The busy sidewalk outside Thurston Court was no place for a toddler. "Okay, we'll walk," she agreed as he hustled toward the entrance. The walls were high, surrounded by thick landscaping, which afforded privacy from the busy commercial district that rimmed the neighborhood. The view was obscured until she was out on the Fifth Avenue sidewalk. Traffic hummed and she gripped his hand tighter.

"We'll stand here for a minute, Tommy Kipnick. First rule of being lost, stay put. You're the findee. We'll wait for the finder."

"Big bus." He swiped his cheek and pointed as a city bus roared past.

"Did you come here on a big bus?"

"Mommy." Mommy was followed by a string of sentences she couldn't make out. She chided herself as she strained to make sense of his chatter. She earned a healthy living catering to the tastes of children and now she was useless to help one terrified lost soul.

"Show me, darling," she tried. Surely he'd tug her hand or lean toward the bus stop or lead her back to an obviously familiar house. She waited, but the child seemed as bewildered as she. Maybe Mommy was out here somewhere, as frantic as she was beginning to feel.

"Okay. We'll stay out there, but I'm going to have to hold you, little guy." She scooped him over her hip. "It's too dangerous—" He silenced her with a wail, locked his small elbows, shoved her at the shoulders and arched backward. Shannon grasped at air as he flipped out of her arms. She crumpled under him, cushioned his fall and landed against the granite curb on her hip—not nearly as well padded as his diapered bottom.

He was out of her arms and racing back into Thurston Court before she regained her balance. "Stop. Don't run," she pleaded as she pressed the pain in her thigh and followed him in a combination limp and power walk. His small legs pumped as he raced ahead of her.

"Stop!"

He stopped, turned and looked up at her frantic expression, then cringed.

"Kip!"

The name was shouted twice behind her, two octaves lower than the "Mommy" piercing the air in front of her. She turned. A six-foot-two-inch version of the child was bearing down on both of them. His own blue eyes were wide and troubled, his hair a match to the towhead's. He tossed a collapsible stroller and backpack at her feet as he tore past her.

Adult and child met at her brick walk. The toddler stopped wailing, but as he looked up his expression changed from pure relief to one even Shannon could read: *Now I'm in big trouble.*

"I want Mommy," the toddler screeched. He scooted backward.

"Watch out for the steps," Shannon called. Too

late. Kipnick whoever-he-was tripped on the bricks and fell spread-eagle across her geraniums.

"Kip!"

Her hip ached and she limped closer as the man scooped the child out of her flowers into a hug. Half a geranium stem packed with smashed coral blooms dangled from the denim seam of the toddler's overalls, then fell on the grass. She didn't dare pick it up. Instead she pressed her hip and held back her dismay only because the two of them seemed so overwhelmed by relief.

"Nicholas." This time it was an apologetic whisper as small arms locked around his neck and the compact little body pressed into his cable-knit sweater. "It's okay, buddy," he murmured. "I was just as scared as you." He sighed and shook his head. "I'm sure not Mommy, am I."

"No, Tendaddy. I want my Mommy," he cried between staggered, hiccupy sobs that finally diminished against his shoulder.

Shannon picked up another broken stem to keep from intruding further on the intimacy of the family drama.

"You're wincing."

She didn't turn until she felt a hand on her shoulder.

"Me?"

"Are you all right?" he was saying. "I saw you fall." Shannon watched him look her over. Their eyes locked briefly before he shifted the child to his other hip. "You saved him from cracking his head open.

Are you hurt? You must be. I'm damned sorry. We were waiting for the bus. He was right beside me while I tried to close the stroller…it jammed.'' He nodded in the direction of the dropped equipment. ''Those things are made for women's hands. I couldn't—I swear I hardly took my eyes— Somebody said he went into the convenience store.'' He sucked in a breath and held it. ''Half the customers are still squatting in the aisles looking for him.'' He sighed again. ''I'm rambling. I'm sorry. He scared the life out of me.''

''I can see that,'' she replied.

His eyes widened.

''Mommy.''

''It's okay.'' He rubbed the small head. ''Kip,'' he whispered and nuzzled. ''He loves buses, so I thought we'd ride out to the zoo. Lord, he was gone in a flash.''

''You shouldn't have let him out of your sight. Fastest thing I've seen on two feet,'' she replied. ''I'll bet he's a handful. I would think a father would know better.''

''He is a handful. I'm sorry. Really.'' There were crimson petals stuck to the toe of his hiking boot. ''He's destroyed your flowers and given you a hell of a limp. You've probably bruised—'' he glanced back at her hips ''—something.''

''I'll heal. I'm Shannon McEvoy, by the way. I just moved in this weekend. I'm glad I was out here gardening instead of unpacking. Your son could have wandered all over the complex.'' He looked stricken and she regretted her tone of voice. "I'm sorry. I didn't mean to preach. I'm sure you were as frightened as he was. I can hardly imagine—"

"Do you have any?" He leaned over and pulled a geranium stem from the toddler's overall strap.

"Children?"

"Sorry. Yes, kids."

"No. He was trying to tell me his name. Kip? Nick?"

His terror-struck expression subsided. Although he looked a far cry from comfortable, his shoulders relaxed as he ruffled the child's hair. "This is Nicholas Goulding." He sucked in another breath and wiped tears from Kip's face with wide sweeps of his thumb. "His mother named him Nicholas after me, but with two of us, it's confusing. When I have him I've been calling him *Kip.*"

"You and—his mother aren't together?"

"No."

"How often is he with you?" He looked startled and she flushed. "I'm sorry. I didn't mean to pry. He just seemed anxious for Mommy, not Tendaddy, or whatever it is he calls you."

He laughed ruefully. "Not often enough. I admit I need practice. I thought the zoo would be a great place to spend the day. Safe. Hassle-free."

"Once you get there."

"Right."

"If he's not used to being called *Kip,* you probably confused him when he got lost." She regretted the comment as he scrutinized her.

"The confusion was mine. I hadn't counted on the stroller, backpack, sunscreen. I'm still rambling. Sorry. My heart's in overdrive."

"So is mine, Mr. Goulding."

"Call me Nick."

"All right, Nick. Kip's a good nickname, once he gets used to it." She smiled at the toddler but he shrank from her and mumbled something that ended in "zoo."

She watched Nick Goulding kiss the child's damp cheeks. "We'll try again." He pulled crumpled bills from his jeans. "For the flowers."

"No, really. Keep the money for the zoo."

"Bus."

The squeal of a Fifth Avenue city bus made them all turn. "Here's our chance and I'll have to run or we'll miss it. Thanks. Thanks again. You sure you won't take the money?"

Shannon shook her head. "Spend it on your adventure."

He stuffed the bills back into his pocket. "I'll make it up to you. I don't have time to argue."

She reached out to pat Nicholas Goulding, the younger, but he shrank back into the masculine hug. Her too-intimate caress landed on the father's shoulder and she was grateful that he ignored it.

"Bus."

"I know, buddy."

He whistled through his teeth with a force that stopped the driver from closing his door and slung the pack over his shoulder. Without further chat, he hustled with the toddler under one arm and the stroller under the other. Shannon watched them go and when Nick turned back, their eyes met. Scrutiny, again. She waved as they climbed the steps.

2

Nick settled Kip next to him on the bus seat and took a final deep breath as his pulse finally slowed. Frantic didn't begin to describe the last ten minutes. Frantic. The word normally wasn't even part of his vocabulary.

And now he was Goulding. He'd thought about the fact that he and Kip had different surnames, of course. What he hadn't considered was how hard it would be to remember. *Nick Goulding.* Damn, he should have practiced it. Sure he was throwing himself into the dating arena to observe eligible women and their reaction to single fathers, but he hadn't counted on his parenting skills being evaluated by nearly six feet of skepticism on his first time out. Shannon McEvoy. He wiped a smudge of her potting soil from Kip's cheek. "What's our game?"

The toddler was back to smiles. "No Nicks."

Nick wagged his finger at his nephew. "No Nicholas here. All I see is Kip."

Kip giggled and wagged his tiny finger back. "No Nick here. I see Tendaddy."

"Good Job," Nick replied as much to himself as

to Kip. Pretend Daddy. The minute Kate and Paul had left, he'd started Kip practicing in the hopes that should they ever need it, the little guy would manage to say some version of Daddy instead of Uncle Nick in the company of the women he planned to observe in the next few days. Nicholas was Kip; he was Daddy. He had no plans to pursue any of the subjects he might meet. Still, introductions were bound to be made and for the next week they were both going to be Nicholas Goulding.

He looked past his nephew and out the window. As the bus pulled away from the curb, the redhead, hand on her bruised hip, knelt to her crushed geraniums. *Shannon McEvoy.* She'd stood there giving him the third degree while those green eyes took in every inch of him. She'd brushed his shoulder. A jolt of desire surprised him.

He leaned back against the seat and savored it. He could have missed the bus. It would have been perfectly logical to linger, help clean up the mess Kip had made, let the chemistry develop. He knew vibes when he felt them. She'd admitted to not having kids and he hadn't seen a wedding ring.

Of course she might have taken it off to do her gardening. One of his best columns was a piece on what he'd called Banded Women. What was a guy to do, he'd written. He knew divorcées who wore bands on their ring fingers, and blissfully married female executives who kept theirs in jewelry boxes. Go figure.

In this case he'd bet money there'd be a flip side

to all that maternal anxiety and concern. She'd asked questions about Kate and questions about how often he had Kip. *Shannon McEvoy.* He glanced at the toddler and tried to remember if he'd mentioned that he—they—lived on Thurston Court as well.

He chided himself for inventing intrigue while he pulled pen and journal from his backpack and opened to page one. His journalistic gut was never wrong. The mishap had the makings of the perfect opening for the article. She had rescued Kip, then eagerly sought information. He could practically see her interest in him rise as she'd pulled clues to his marital status out of the conversation. Hadn't she asked about Kate and how often he had Kip? Of course he'd change the location, her name and physical description. In his head he was already embellishing the episode as he scribbled in the notebook.

It was nearly five o'clock by the time Shannon salvaged what was left of her geraniums and got out of the shower. She was no stranger to parents and their children. What she observed in her shop could fill a chapter on parenting. The last time she'd seen a handsome six-footer come unglued, he'd been a customer with a three-year-old bent on handling some of her most delicate dollhouse pieces at Time Out. By the time Shannon had come from behind the counter, the temper tantrum had reduced two of her reproduction canopy beds and a dining room chair to kindling.

Comparatively, the two Nicholas Gouldings had been positively endearing. Yet she didn't smile. Divorce was traumatic enough without being called one name by your mother and another by your father. Surely they could agree on that much. Again she reran the conversation through her head. He hadn't mentioned divorce. He hadn't even referred to Kip's mother as his ex-wife. Maybe they'd never married. In this day and age, anything was possible.

Although Kip couldn't have been lost for more than minutes, it was easy to imagine Nick's agony. The toddler's desperate hug had made her wince, yet it was Nicholas, senior, who kept popping into her head. His anguish still tore at her heart and made her ache as much as patting the bruise under her towel.

"Even with the bus waiting he looked frantic. Backpack probably jammed with diapers, the half-collapsed stroller and the little guy clinging to his neck for dear life... Nicholas Goulding, the elder, needs practice venturing out alone with Nicholas Goulding, the younger." Shannon laughed as she described the mishap and offered her half brother the last of the delicatessen dinner he'd brought with him.

She and Evan shared the McEvoy height and easy temperament but they each resembled their mothers. Her father's first wife had been of Italian descent. Evan was dark with a straight Roman nose and square jaw. Shannon carried the Celtic genes of both her parents, from her fair complexion to the flaming tangle of lustrous hair.

Evan stabbed a marinated tortellini. "Did you get a good look at him standing up?"

"He was on his feet the whole time, why?" She narrowed her gaze. "Oh, no, you don't."

"Sounds like a six-footer."

"Sounds like a direct lead-in to speculation on my social life."

"What social life? You're having takeout salads with your brother on a Saturday night."

"One I'm not likely to tell you about."

"My mistake. I've been here an hour and *Nick Goulding* keeps floating off your tongue as though the guy offers possibilities."

Self-preservation kicked in. "For your information, Mr. Goulding came up to my chin. His wedding band ran from knuckle to knuckle and he couldn't have been more than twenty-two or twenty-three years old. He explained that his wife calls the baby Nicholas and he calls him Kip. The guy's short, married and young." She lied about all three over the last of the sesame noodles. "Now stop giving me that incorrigibly smug expression."

Her brother stretched his legs out under the table and arched an eyebrow.

Nick started up Shannon McEvoy's front walk with a cardboard box of geranium flats in his arms and repeated glances over his shoulder. He'd parked his four-by-four at the curb for an unrestricted view of the toddler. Kip was asleep in his car seat—for the moment. Damned if he didn't want to crawl into bed himself. Rowing the entire Allegheny didn't take this much energy.

As he rang the bell he glanced through the curtainless bay window. Shannon was standing in it. He gazed at her, assessing her striking features. Her hair was pulled back at the temples from high cheekbones, her full lips were pursed, and he lingered over the green eyes that had worked him over as he'd spit out his unrehearsed explanations. She turned and brushed back the loose coppery curls that touched the shoulders of her shirt, some shimmery thing that held the light as she moved a lamp. His reaction was even stronger than it had been that afternoon.

Although it was barely dusk, a brass chandelier illuminated the cozy niche, a variation of his sister and brother-in-law's at the other end of the curved street. The table was set with the remains of dinner. His stomach growled.

Shannon bent down and plugged in the lamp. He saw her wince and rub her hip. Her shirt was tucked into khaki shorts tied with a drawstring that emphasized her narrow waist. She stood and snapped on the lamp. Light played off the shirt and the crown of her hair as she ran her hands through it. Poise. Even her afternoon fall had been graceful. Damn his reverie. He'd met and observed women all afternoon, chatted with a few, watched them kneel and fawn over Kip, scribbled notes out of sight, kept right on course.

Okay, so the course had wound its way back to the McEvoy brick walk. He felt like a Peeping Tom as he damned the lies and assumptions that he'd concocted to pull off the project. Damn his pulse, his stomach and every other part of him that was reacting

to a simple glimpse through a window. Worry over
Kip was not what drove his heart against his ribs now.

Her breasts and hips moved under her clothes, giving the fabric life. She could have been gliding down
a runway or gracefully rowing a shell through the
water. She was built for both. Studying her reaction
to him was one thing. His reaction to her was something else altogether. Three Thurston Court was too
close for comfort. The last thing he needed this week
was the complication of his sister's green-eyed gar-
dener of a neighbor. Maybe he should move Kip over
to the island and into his condo. There was little
chance he'd run her into out there—unless she was a
rower. Hell, she had the height and the grace for the
sport. On the other hand, Pittsburgh's entire rowing
community from high school and collegiate teams to
the senior recreational clubs used the joint facilities
of one boathouse. This was not a woman he would
have missed if she had anything to do with his sport.

Nick took a deep breath and let it out slowly. Forget the doorbell. He had the rest of the summer to
walk this slippery path. Anonymous or otherwise,
she'd been his first subject and a good one. Strike
that. A great one. Any pursuit of Shannon McEvoy
would have to wait until he was back to his normal
routine.

Without ringing the bell again, he set the geraniums
on the doorstep where she'd find them in the morning,
but as he started to leave, the door opened. His grin
faded as a guy as casually dressed as Shannon stepped
over the threshold. "Yes?"

He didn't know whether to be relieved or disappointed. "Geraniums. I'm Nick. Goulding." He stuck out his hand under sudden intense examination. "I didn't mean to bother you. I'm just replacing the flats—"

"You're Nick Goulding?"

"Yes." They shook hands.

"Evan McEvoy. Sorry if I was staring. You're not exactly the way Shannon described you." He finally looked at the box. "I heard about your son and the flowers."

"Shannon told you?"

He laughed. "She made it all sound like Laurel and Hardy. Come on in."

A husband. Just as well. Nick motioned to the car. "Can't. I just wanted to drop off some replacements with a final apology." He shifted from one boot to the other as the scrutiny continued.

"Let me at least get Shannon. She'll want to thank you."

"Just tell her..." Evan had already disappeared, leaving the door ajar.

Nick glanced down the hall past stacked boxes, some open, some still sealed. The foyer opened into the living room where a rug lay rolled up in front of a couch. Shannon's voice drifted from inside and then she appeared, crossing in front of the couch and hurrying toward him barefoot with long, easy strides.

"Nick." She smiled as she reached the door. Second time. Second thunder. Her eyes were wide with what might be pleasant surprise. She glanced at the flowers. "Evan said you brought geraniums. How nice. This wasn't necessary at all."

"It's the least I could do."

"I know they were flattened, but I cut back the stems. They'll be fine. Lots of new growth in no time."

"Bloom about August?"

She smiled. "You're right. I guess I could use some fresh ones. Thank you. You even matched the color. Thank you. I'll plant them tomorrow. Come in, please. We were just about to have coffee."

He shook his head as a howl sailed through the Jeep's open window. "I'm being paged." He looked over his shoulder. "Long day."

"How was the zoo?"

"Fun. Kip thought it was almost as much of an adventure as riding the bus. He could have ridden Pittsburgh's transit system all afternoon. I had to pry him out of his seat with promises of lions and tigers."

"No more tears?"

"Not a peep out of him the whole time, which you probably don't believe now. I'm sorry he's started up again."

"Must be me."

"His guardian angel? Better not be you. No, he's tuckered out, that's all. I finally got the foolish stroller set up but I couldn't keep him in it for more than five minutes. He's been on his feet as long as I have."

She smiled that smile. "After all that I hope you didn't drag him all over the place looking for the flowers."

He looked at them and shook his head. "No. We just picked them up at the garden center on Beechwood. Long day, that's all. Kip's legs finally gave out and the crib's calling. Thanks—thanks again for this afternoon."

"You're welcome. But I'm no guardian angel." She glanced over his shoulder and laughed. "He's the angel. You'd better get him home."

"Right." He swore he felt her eyes on him all the way down the walk. His nape and that spot between his shoulder blades were never wrong. He started the ignition and when she was still on her porch with the box in her arms, her husband came back out. Nick ignored the stab of disappointment. A husband settled all the issues, including the proximity of their addresses. All for the better. Let the journalistic wheels get spinning. In true Jake O'Donnell style he could turn the fact that she was married into a feckless observation, maybe something about the difficulty of separating the wheat from the chaff.

"I'm glad I was here to help," she called.

Nick drove around the horseshoe bend in the housing complex and tried to decide if he were glad as well.

At five-fifteen Monday evening Shannon grabbed a shopping cart and pushed it along the dairy aisle as she glanced at her shopping list. It wasn't her usual shopping hour. One of Jake O'Donnell's "Since You Asked" columns had been devoted to the theory that the grocery store in early evening was a great place

for guys to meet single professional women.
O'Donnell's usual sardonic wit and cockeyed view of
the world had made her feel like an overripe tomato
in the produce section, desperate to be chosen for
someone's garden salad. She'd tried to avoid the dinner hour since she'd read it. Five o'clock was on the
early side, she hoped. Desperate she certainly was not.

Between the weekend unpacking and gardening
and all day today back at her Walnut Street toy shop,
there was still little in her kitchen cupboards but pasta
and cereals.

She thought about Jake O'Donnell's column as she
wheeled down the dairy aisle. He'd described single
women with his usual predatory implication that desperate unmarried females put in a full day's work,
then parked themselves in the fresh produce aisle of
their neighborhood grocery chain stores in the hopes
that Mr. Right would be stopping off for a head of
lettuce on his way home, too. The gall.

It might interest Mr. O'Donnell to know that her
evening was going to be devoted to arranging her
purchases and planting the flat of geraniums Nick had
dropped off. Furthermore, she was looking forward to
both activities. She was here to get familiar with the
layout of this particular neighborhood grocery chain
store because it was the closest. She'd pick up staples
to stock her new kitchen, and grab something ready-
made from the deli for a light supper. Simple as that.

Guardian angel. Shannon grabbed individual con-
tainers of yogurt. She tried to concentrate on getting

her bearings instead of the fact that Nick Goulding kept floating around in her head as unexpectedly as both of his arrivals on her doorstep. She'd already endured a solid round of teasing from Evan, who'd demanded to know why she had lied about everything from his height to his age.

She reached for a quart of low-fat milk. Why had she? Because he was too attractive? Too personable? Too— She didn't know what, couldn't even name what it was that had kept him in the forefront of her consciousness since their first encounter. Yes she could.

She made a U-turn with her cart. Chemistry, pure and simple. Animal magnetism. She'd felt it and she'd bet her shop's next shipment of imported hand puppets that he'd felt it, too. Handsome and hapless. Men as well put together as Nick Goulding were never desperate or anxious, or—saints above—vulnerable. Men that well turned out were confident to the teeth. Arrogant, most of them; heartbreakers all. That's why there was something so disconcerting about this one, unstrung by the antics of a toddler. She felt like butter left too close to the stove.

Butter. She grabbed a pound and searched for the cheeses. Daydreaming about Nick Goulding wasn't going to steer her cart. She cleared her head. Pay attention; study these unfamiliar shelves; get your bearings, she ordered. When she'd found the feta, grated Parmesan and some Swiss, she wheeled her cart to the end of the aisle and pivoted around the next one. Nick Goulding stood halfway down the aisle with Kip perched in the seat of his shopping cart. Her insides went back to melted butter.

He had on jeans again and a simple polo shirt nearly the color of his eyes. She smiled—felt the grin break right out at the same moment her heart jumped. She hadn't realized she remembered the color of his eyes. But one glance at the shirt had brought it back. His eyes were blue, clear and dark, and dead-on honest. She'd already glimpsed fear, relief and open curiosity. Yesterday's confrontation had been about as straightforward as it gets.

Father and son were in front of the cereal display. Kip was in the cart seat digging through a box of animal crackers, swinging his legs. His left foot was clad in the sneaker he'd worn the day before. Kip's right foot was only covered in a sock.

Shannon held back. Nick looked a little befuddled as he scanned the shelves. He knelt, then stood, then leaned to Kip, who was trying to stand in his seat. A handful of crackers fell on the floor. As Nick scooped them up, a woman who had been at the far end of the aisle left her cart and knelt with him.

Shannon was too far out of earshot to hear anything, but the woman pointed to the shelves, then stood up and took a box of cereal and handed it to Nick. Even half an aisle away Shannon recognized the box. It was plain old cornflakes. Surely he could have found that by himself.

The women smiled and self-consciously fingered her blond bangs. She ruffled Kip's hair; Kip pushed her hand away. It could have been worse, Shannon wanted to tell her. The little guy could have arched backward, as desperate as he'd been yesterday to get away from an unfamiliar touch.

The chatting continued and the woman seemed in no hurry to get back to her own needs. A pang of something close to jealousy registered in Shannon's chest. Jealousy? Her stomach growled and she steered the cart toward the deli counter to pick out some dinner.

There was more of a wait than she'd anticipated. The half-dozen customers placing their orders for salads and lunch meats seemed to be entirely women, some young enough to be area college students, some close to retirement. She tried not to think about Jake O'Donnell's theories.

It was ten minutes before she placed her order and as she took her container of chicken salad, the blonde wheeled in next to her. Attractive; thirty something; ringless left hand. Jake O'Donnell had written about that, too. One of his more amusing columns.

Shannon wheeled her cart along the back wall to the meat section and spotted Kip's tiny sneaker as she approached the chicken. Providence. Sooner or later he'd be searching the aisles himself for the missing shoe. She put packages of poultry and a lean cut of beef into the cart and started another search down each aisle. She found father and son in the dry goods, parked in front of the diapers and baby wipes. A brunette in her late twenties with nothing but a handheld basket was nodding enthusiastically over the box of diapers she held. With a final smile and a sort of cooing expression for Kip, she dropped the parcel into Nick's cart. Again? The man was a magnet.

Shannon waited long enough to make sure she wouldn't interrupt, then started down the aisle as the woman left. As she approached, Nick took a small notebook out of his hip pocket and began to scribble. He seemed to sense something and turned. She hadn't seen the full gambit of Goulding expressions after all. His eyebrows arched. He shoved the notebook into his hip pocket and—she couldn't swear to it—appeared to blush. By the time she was within earshot, his complexion was normal. She held out the shoe. "I hope I wasn't interrupting anything. I thought you might be looking for this."

"Shannon."

"You seemed to be taking notes." She grinned at his discomfort.

"Grocery list," he muttered and looked at the child. "Hard to concentrate with my helper along. Look, Kip, Shannon found your sneaker." Nick looked at the little boy who was still busy with his box of animal crackers.

"I spotted it in the meat section and thought it looked familiar."

"Thanks, I hadn't had the time… We were about to go look for it." He took it and leaned to Kip's foot. It immediately became a game. Kip yanked his foot up, Nick grabbed and stuffed. "It fit this morning," he muttered as the toddler curled his tiny toes in defiance and laughed his toddler laugh. He kicked. As crackers spilled down the bib of his overalls, he managed to pop the sneaker from the end of his foot into the air. It bounced neatly off Shannon's shoulder.

"Hold it right there, Cinder-fella." She laughed as she took his socked foot and firmly eased his toes back into the shoe. "Here you go. Perfect fit." She expected tears again, but Kip looked up and smiled instead, exposing a mouthful of gooey cookie crumbs.

"Guardian angel and now Prince-ess Charming," Nick said.

Shannon glanced at him. "There seems to be no shortage of princesses around here at this hour. I hate to admit it, but Jake O'Donnell might have been onto something."

Nick's complexion darkened again. "Jake O'Donnell?"

"The column that ran last fall…his theory that the grocery store at the dinner hour is a great place for meeting women. Single women. You seem to be attracting your share."

A single brow arched again. "Had me under surveillance?"

She shrugged. "Been trying to find a minute when I wouldn't be interrupting."

"Jake O'Donnell fan, are you?"

"Hardly."

"Read him much?"

"His column comes in handy for wrapping fish and holding my potting soil. I'm hardly alone in that view, but of course, a writer like O'Donnell probably thrives on the righteous indignation of his female readers."

He was fighting a grin. "Female righteous indignation. I like that. You think the column has many female readers?"

"Originally? Not when it ran deep in the sports pages next to the football scores."

"You found it scanning the football scores?"

"I have three older brothers."

"I guess that's explanation enough."

"I'm sure some brilliant editor moved it to the lifestyle pages where he knew it would raise ire, dander and outrage."

"Astute observation for someone who wraps fish in it."

She narrowed her glance. "Are you laughing at me?"

"I wouldn't dare." He cocked his head. "The column was moved about two years ago. I got the impression you guys were new to Pittsburgh."

"I'm new to Thurston Court and the city proper. I've been living out in Mount Lebanon in the apartment over Evan's garage while I got my business established. I own a toy shop on Walnut Street. I teach crafts there, too, and puppet making, making dollhouse miniatures, whatever happens to be hot at the moment."

"Back up to the part about Evan's garage. Where was Evan?"

"In the house with his family."

"You're not family?"

"Of course. He's my half brother." She cocked her head. "Who did you think he was?"

"A husband. I just assumed when he answered the door—"

"Didn't he introduce himself?"

"As Evan McEvoy, sure."

It suddenly seemed important to explain Evan's marital situation, the fact that Jeannie and the girls were at the McEvoy family cottage out at Lake Scituate and that she'd asked him to dinner since work had kept him in the city for the weekend. "Evan's my brother. Half brother to be precise. You couldn't see the resemblance? Probably not. We both favor our mothers. Nina McEvoy died when he was a toddler, leaving Dad with three boys. For some reason Mom found a widower struggling with three irrepressible kids irresistible. Not unlike some of your eager volunteers in here tonight." Nick suddenly busied himself with Kip, who was now offering up his empty box of crackers. "Anyway, they added me to round out the family and that's my life story. One more sentence and Kip'll be out on the floor." She nodded at her cart and sighed. "I've spent so much time returning the sneaker and describing the McEvoy family tree, I haven't finished my own list." She leaned to the toddler. "Keep your shoes on." He fussed and she tousled his hair, but he didn't seem to mind.

3

Shannon McEvoy was single, not only single but begrudgingly familiar with "Since You Asked" and Jake O'Donnell. Even as Nick settled Kip into his high chair and set dinner on the tray, he was still mulling over the conversation. Rarely did any woman make him self-conscious. Hell, when was the last time some levelheaded female had his heart thundering against his ribs in the midst of the produce aisle? It had been an hour since he'd left the grocery store and he still couldn't decide if he'd been glad to see her again or not.

Single. All that wide-eyed concern, compassion and wit, not to mention the package it was wrapped in, was unencumbered by a husband. Suddenly Subject Number One was back in the article in the pure, humorous way he'd envisioned. There was humor, irony, pathos—especially if he confessed to the terror of losing a child in a crowd, and the unbridled relief at finding a statuesque, flaming-haired guardian angel at the end of her front walk. Okay, he'd change the location and make her a perky little blonde to safeguard her identity. The lead was already strong and with a little polish and irreverence, he'd make the mishap the stuff of prizewinning journalism.

So far he'd been right on the nose with his predictions. A toddler in the cart and a few helpless glances at the grocery shelves had brought women of every description to his aid. Almost as many as had struck up conversations at the zoo. No doubt a puppy would have worked as well, but until golden retrievers were allowed in the shopping carts, a toddler would have to do. And Kip was doing nicely.

"Dinner, Tendaddy."

"Dinner it is." The term Tendaddy had stuck and not once had Kip done the unthinkable and wailed, "You're not my daddy," in public.

Nick sat down next to the high chair. They were on Kate's front yard patio, hidden from the lane by an ivy-covered wall. Access from the house was through French doors in the dining room. Right where Shannon has her bay window, he thought absently as he handed Kip mashed green beans.

While Kip worked tiny bits of finger food into his mouth, Nick flipped the pages of his small spiral notebook with his thumb and read over his notes. It wasn't Kip and his dinner antics that ruined his concentration. Shannon popped into his head. Shannon grinning as she handed him the sneaker; Shannon with her head cocked in that way she had as she'd teased him about the other women; Shannon with her eyes shining as she described her brothers. Shannon—unmarried.

"More."

He reached for the peach slices on the glass-topped table. He had a deadline, one he wasn't about to muck up because a green-eyed redhead made his adrenaline surge. A good row on the Allegheny could do that.

While Kip worked the peaches into his mouth, Nick began to formulate a new tone for his piece. Dan Miller and Charlie Hutchinson expected the magazine article to be in Jake O'Donnell's style. The thought exhausted him. Once he'd finished the research, it was time to bring Nicholas Hansen to the fore. Irony, humor; *Three Rivers Magazine* had a sophisticated readership. A little self-deprecating humor would work nicely with the upscale readers who would be—hopefully—chuckling right along with him at the theory and proof of the frailty of women from a bachelor's point of view.

And hadn't Shannon shown up again, this time sneaker in hand? When he least expected it, there she was, in the midst of his research, coming to the rescue. He smiled and wiped Kip's chin. Of course finding a lost shoe didn't have quite the edge of finding a lost child, but he could make it work. No matter how he wound up describing her in print, the Shannon McEvoy episodes would add depth to the piece. "I've got the opening I was looking for, Kip, thanks to your guardian angel."

When this foolish experiment was over he wouldn't mind some Shannon McEvoy episodes in his personal life, as well. For now he had to toe the line and behave like an aging sociologist if he wanted to get the grist for his acerbic mill. Any woman who raised his hormone level as fast as she did belonged at arm's length. After Charlie Hutchinson had approved his article—

"All done, Tendaddy."

He glanced at Kip. Peach juice glistened on his cheeks. Shredded chicken clung to the hair over his right ear and milk dripped from the lip of the tray onto the flagstone. "Not by a long shot, kiddo. There's a bath calling." As soon as he put Kip to bed, he'd call his sister and brother-in-law for their daily update, then he'd hit the computer and rework his data. Humor would carry the article. He was sure of it.

An hour later, with the bath, diaper, pajamas, picture book and prayers conquered, Nick stood in Kip's darkened doorway and watched his nephew's newly angelic form under the glow of the night-light. His early tears for Daddy and Mommy had finally been replaced by his small bear hugs and grins and games the two of them invented as they made it through the day. Nick still made his daily promised reports to Kate and Paul after Kip's bedtime, however, to maintain the hard-won peace.

Nick yawned and quietly closed the door, no longer surprised at the surge of affection and pride that prickled his skin. He'd be thirty-two in October. It was time, his sister, Kate, was only too fond of reminding him, that he committed to something besides rowing shells and journalistic deadlines. His instant reply had always been that Kip satisfied all his paternal instincts, but as he went down the stairs, he admitted to himself there'd be plenty he was going to miss when the week was over, despite the chaos and unending responsibility.

He was heading for the laundry room to strip out of his peach, green bean, baby shampoo and bathwater soaked shirt when the doorbell sounded. He opened the door to five feet ten inches of turned-out redhead.

"Don't look so shocked, Nick Goulding." She was wagging her finger at him. "Why didn't you tell me you lived right on Winchester Place? For heaven's sake, I've hardly had time to explore all these back cul-de-sacs, so you can imagine my surprise when I spotted your four-by-four, baby seat and all, as I came around the bend just now. In fact, the high chair on the patio was a dead giveaway."

"Dining alfresco has its advantages. I can hose everything down."

She laughed but his pulse gave a panicked leap as she looked past him, into the living room. "Your layout is quite similar to mine. Why didn't you tell me we were neighbors?" She cocked her head. "Are you hiding something?"

Hiding something? Hell, he wasn't going to touch that one with a ten-foot sculling oar. He tried to catch his breath and laugh with her. She'd pinned up her hair and thrown on a sweater, but it was the same breezy, laughing, green-eyed Shannon he'd left at the checkout line. He was staring and he knew it. Before he could think of an alibi, she tapped his chest.

"Mashed green beans?" She laughed, then pulled

his soaking sleeve away from his shoulder. "You've either washed the car or washed that toddler." She dropped her voice to a whisper. "Am I being too loud? Is Kip asleep?"

She wasn't being too much of anything except irresistible. "No and yes," he managed to say. Desire danced through the length of him.

She was looking over his shoulder again, to the left, but this time her expression softened. Her smile flickered. He followed her glance to the end table next to the couch, knowing full well what had caught her attention. Kate and Kip grinned from an eight-by-ten photo next to the lamp. Beside it was a photo he'd taken and given to Paul for Christmas: Kate in a sundress hiked to her shins as she kicked her bare foot in the inlet stream that ran through their family property at High Pines.

"Kip's mother?" she asked gently.

"Yes. That's Kate." There. Absolute truth, but his pulse still jumped. If Shannon stepped four feet farther in, she'd see the table at the far end of the couch, chock-full of framed shots of Paul, Kip and Kate as the happy trio.

In self-defense he put his arm around her shoulder, ignoring the fact that he'd spread peaches onto her sweater. "I guess I just didn't think to mention my address," he admitted. "Running into you has always been so frantic. Too rushed...worried about Kip... you know how it's been." He started to steer her to the right, through the dining area toward the kitchen. "How about some ice cream? I've got some

Strawberry Swirl and Dutch Chocolate in the freezer. Cup of coffee? Beer?'' He regretted the offer the moment he'd made it. The refrigerator door was a veritable gallery of Goulding snapshots. He stopped abruptly at the edge of the table to keep her from the kitchen. Shannon bumped closer, a perfect fit in the crook of his arm. He had to fight the urge to tug her into a full embrace.

She was the one to finally back up, as if she needed to look him squarely in the eye with that deep, penetrating glance. ''Nothing, thanks,'' she murmured. ''I can't stay. I just rang the bell to satisfy my curiosity.''

He guided her the few steps back to the front door and opened it. She smiled. ''Since you live this close, if I'm not being too presumptuous, could I borrow Kip for a little bit tomorrow evening after I get home from the shop? Believe it or not, I could use the little guy's help. I'd like to let him play with some puppets I'm thinking of selling. I'd like to see how durable they are and whether or not they're too sophisticated for his age group. I'd have you bring him by the store, but it would be too hectic with customers and other distractions.''

He knew all about distraction.

''I'll give the two of you a quick dinner as a thank-you. Nothing elaborate. We could do it early. I can be home by five-thirty.''

''At your place?''

She smiled again. ''Number three. The one with the geraniums. You'd be doing me a big favor.''

She waited. Stood there with that glance turning him inside out. Drum up an excuse. Put it off till the damned article's finished and the experiment's over, he told himself. Keep this five foot ten inches of temptation at arm's length.

"Tomorrow night would be fine," he replied as if someone else were answering for him.

"Wonderful. Alfresco, too. My little patio's in the back. Kip will like the courtyard."

"I'll bring some toys to keep him occupied."

"That would be nice." She went down one step, then stopped and gave him that look again. His gut tightened. "Nick, those photographs in the other room—I've assumed you were divorced."

"Yes." Yes as in *continue,* he should have explained.

She was already adding, "But you've kept the pictures of your wife in such a prominent place. Your ex-wife."

"For Kip," he replied lamely.

"Are you a widower?"

Oh, God. That assumption had never occurred to him. Nothing much logical and clearheaded occurred to him when Shannon McEvoy stood this close. "No. No, I'm not. Kate's very much alive. It's complicated, Shannon. I'd like to leave it at that."

Now he'd embarrassed her. She brushed his damp sleeve again, obviously flustered. "Of course. I didn't mean to pry. Go get out of that green beans and bubble bath."

She was gone before more small talk mired him

any deeper. His pulse was pounding; his adrenaline had his heart in his throat. How had he gotten himself into this mess? He watched her walk toward the bend in the lane, watched her sweater catch the light and loose strands of hair bounce softly on her shoulder. She tucked a bit back up into her barrette as she walked, as if she sensed that his eyes had never left her. Was the sensation as intense as what he'd felt under her scrutiny Sunday evening?

Nick turned around, leaned against his sister's door frame and stared into the living room. Why hadn't he said that this was Kate's house? These were Kip's digs and he was here while Kate was away. Fact, every innocent word. He should at least have told Shannon that much of the truth.

Shannon let her assistant finish the day and left Walnut Street at four o'clock Tuesday afternoon. She grinned sheepishly as she glanced at the puppets she'd placed on her kitchen counter. She had any number of subjects willing to try out toys, from her young customers to the children of her friends. Okay, she admitted it—only to herself. Kip and the puppets had been a gimmick to get Nick Goulding to dinner.

The more she saw of him, the more fascinated she became. He was reticent, she thought as she crumbled feta cheese into a mixed salad. She'd hit a nerve last night with her prying, but it had been necessary. In the grocery store he'd done nothing to dissuade every interested woman in the building from striking up a conversation. An hour later shock had stiffened every inch of her. It wasn't just the photographs that screamed *married*. Nick Goulding didn't seem to be the type to choose ruffled swags at the kitchen window or flowered chintz on the dining-room chair seats.

She reassured herself that the feminine ambience was countered by the honesty in those wide, dark eyes, the faint flush that dusted his cheeks and his sweet ineptness with Kip. Nick Goulding's parenting skills screamed part-time father. She had treaded on sensitive territory but his taciturn behavior brought out the detective in her. He was an enigma.

By five o'clock she had the simple dinner ready. Pittsburgh held the heat and there was enough left in the June evening that warranted her wearing a simple white knit top over silky rayon culottes. She'd washed her hair that morning and it fell to her shoulders, with one side tucked neatly behind her ear. Understated, she hoped, like the man himself.

The Goulding condo was around the bend and down the end of the cul-de-sac, a healthy walk for toddler legs. A night this nice might have Nick pushing Kip in his stroller. She was anxious, hoped she didn't look it, and decided this might be the perfect time to water her clay pots by the front door. Deadheading her front walk flowers might make her appear more relaxed than she felt.

She tipped the watering can and watched the pattern as moisture darkened the terra cotta and drizzled over the bricks. When she straightened up, Nick was at the curb. No Kip. The only thing in his hands was a bottle of wine. Lord, what that man did for a pair of khakis, she thought as she waved. Tonight his shirt was a summery shade of green.

"Nick." A smile burst from her. There was no way to stop it. She craned her neck. "We're missing someone."

He shrugged. "I got a sitter."

Her heart leapt. "No Kip?"

"He's exhausted and cranky, sure to ruin even a quick dinner. I suppose I should have called and told you. Can the puppets wait? I could bring him by the shop tomorrow."

The puppets. "Don't worry. I can find someone else."

"I've got the sitter till nine. If I share a bottle of very ordinary Beaujolais with you will you feed me?"

"Desperate?" She laughed. "Kip's in good hands?"

"He's with one of his regulars, a teenager from next door."

"You're sure you want to stay?"

"That's why I didn't call. You could have turned me down over the phone, but I thought you'd be too polite to send me home once I walked all the way down here."

"It's hardly more than a block or two." It wasn't silly banter she was after and she didn't wait for a reply. "Nick, I'm very confused."

He nodded and looked surprisingly solemn. "We can run it around out here on the front walk or back on that courtyard you mentioned last night."

She nodded toward the front door. "Follow me."
He did and her scalp tingled as it had when she'd left
his condo last night.

"Excuse the clutter." She led him into the foyer
identical to his.

"I know about clutter."

She stepped forward, or maybe he did. All she
knew was that she was back snuggled into him and
the arm slung breezily across her shoulder felt wonderful.

"How tall are you, five-ten?" he asked without
missing a beat as they passed the dining table. He
glanced at stacked plates and an open box that still
contained cookbooks.

"Just about. And you? Six feet? Six-one?" Did she
sound casual?

"Close enough. And you're a perfect fit."

Her scalp tingled as she became aware of every
place their bodies touched.

"You'd make one heck of a rower."

"So I've been told. I've looked into it."

"I've rowed since high school. I'd remember if I'd
ever seen you at the boathouse."

"No time." She shrugged, which gave her the excuse of keeping tucked into his arm. "Or maybe no
discipline. Dawn, Nick. You people row at indecent
hours. Besides, being in business for myself keeps me
hopping. Literally sometimes."

"A sunrise on the Allegheny can get you through
the whole day," he replied. They were in the kitchen.
He put down the bottle and turned back to her. She

stood still with her fair complexion in ruins. Flushes
crept up her neck and over her cheekbones. She could
feel all of it and her mouth went dry under his scrutiny.

"The wine needs a little chilling," she managed to
say.

"And so do I," she thought he murmured.

She put the bottle in an ice bucket and filled it with
a handful of ice cubes and tap water, then turned to
face him across the small breakfast nook. He picked
up one of the puppets she'd laid out for Kip.

"Your place is a nearly identical layout to Kate's."

"Kate's? The one I found you in last night? Nick,
you're sending out very mixed signals, if I may be
blunt." Her attempt at nonchalance included pulling
two wineglasses from the cabinet. "I realize I'm getting personal—" she laid some crackers on a plate
next to raw vegetables "—this is hardly a date. Nev-
ertheless, you can't blame me." She worked the little
bowl of dip into the middle. "I've run into my share
of devious men."

She shot him a glance that she hoped was unset-
tling. "At about the same spot you put your arm
around me here, you put your arm around me at your
place. Last night it was to deftly steer me away from
the photos in the living room." The comment brought
the results she'd hoped for. Discomfort played across
his features. "Nick, if you aren't married, you must
have gotten the house in the settlement and she must
have left about two days ago. That was no bachelor

pad, unless I'm completely misreading you. This would be a very good time to tell me the truth.''

''I'm not married.'' He wagged his left ring finger. ''Scout's honor.''

Scout's honor. She led the way out to the wrought-iron table and chairs on the small patio enclosed by a lattice topped board fence. ''An empty ring finger is hardly proof of anything. Jake O'Donnell wrote a hilarious column on men trying to figure out women's marital status by their ring fingers. When did we women ever have a fair shake in that department? A man's empty ring finger isn't indicative of anything.'' She pulled the corkscrew from her pocket and handed it to him, then set down the hors d'oeuvres.

''You find Jake O'Donnell hilarious?''

''Rarely. Once in a while he points a humorous spin on something a woman can appreciate. He had a point that time. Not that I'm sympathetic to the plight of single men on the prowl.''

''And do you run into many men on the prowl? You don't strike me as the type to be out scrutinizing ring fingers.''

She arched an eyebrow. ''I think we're off the subject.''

He kept a blank expression as he wound the screw and withdrew the cork. There was a soft pop. He poured a glass and handed it to her. ''What was the subject?''

While she sipped, she raised her hand and waved her own empty ring finger.

Nick leaned forward in his chair. ''Shannon, I

swear I'm single.'' He sipped and swallowed. ''And I know you're confused. What I didn't make clear is that the condo isn't mine. The photos of Kate are there because it's hers.''

Something in her began to soften. ''Kate's house. If it's that simple why didn't you say something yesterday?''

''It didn't occur to me. I didn't realize what you were thinking. Kate and her husband Paul are on a quick vacation. I moved in to take care of Kip this week on his own turf. Easier on him.''

''That can't have been easy for you.'' Shannon replied as his expression grew positively endearing. ''Was it ever yours? Did the two of you ever live there together?''

''Thurston Court? No. No we never did.''

''You seem to always be thinking of what's best for your little guy. You are very thoughtful. How thoughtful for your ex-wife, too.'' Almost unconsciously Shannon mimicked his body language and leaned forward as well. The wine sent a comfortable warmth through her, very comfortable.

''Yes. Kate's a great mother.'' He refilled their glasses and ate a cracker. ''Delicious.''

She was beginning to feel delicious herself. ''Does Kip go to day care while you work? Does Kate normally have a nanny for him during the day?''

''Neither. She's a full-time mom and I've taken the week off to be with him while she's away.''

''You're a good father. This all seems so—'' She shrugged. ''I don't know, congenial. Civilized.''

"Congenial and civilized, that we are."

"For your son's sake, I'm sorry your marriage didn't work out."

He winced and dunked a broccoli flowerette into the dip and chewed, then followed it with a baby carrot. "I'd like to change the subject."

"Of course. I shouldn't have gotten so personal." She leaned back in her chair, embarrassed.

He commented on her gas grill at the edge of the patio. Take the hint, she told herself. Nick Goulding, with a few free hours, didn't come down here to be badgered by questions about a failed marriage—or fatherhood, for that matter.

They set the chicken breasts on the grill and she left him in charge and went back to the kitchen for the plate of pepper slices to be added at the last minute. While she was inside, she ran the faucet and stuck her wrists under the cold water. It had been her grandmother's trick for cooling off on sweltering summer days. Parts of her were sweltering now, parts she had no business thinking about with Nick on the other side of the screen door. She could have used Kip.

She returned to the grill and over the sizzle and aroma of her homemade barbecue sauce tried to get the conversation going again. "You know all about my toy business. What do you do, Nick, when you're not taking the week off to be Father of the Year?"

He stabbed the chicken and turned it, then sipped his wine. "What do I do? For the next couple of weeks you could say I'm involved in some research, some sociological work, actually. A study of sorts."

"Fascinating. Are you with one of the colleges? My brother's in the engineering department at CMU."

"Evan?"

She shook her head. "Jeff. He started out at Bucknell but joined the faculty at Carnegie Mellon about five years ago. That's part of the reason I'm in Pittsburgh. I went to Chatham College here—an art major. With two brothers in town, they convinced me to settle back in the 'burgh, as they say. How'd we get back on the subject of me?" She motioned that the chicken needed another basting as she set the peppers on the grill. "You're very good at that."

"Nothing too tough about flipping barbecued chicken."

"I meant at refocusing the conversation."

"Am I?"

"A true sociologist."

He shrugged. "I just don't feel like talking about my work on my time off. Dry stuff. Very dry. Sociology can be deadly dull and confidential, to be honest. It's a study for another party. I'm doing observation and analysis at the moment. Confidential."

"Sounds intriguing."

They stood shoulder to shoulder, staring at the grill as if barbecuing chicken and roasting red peppers were the most fascinating pastimes in the universe. Sparks, warmth, heat was coming at her from all sides, from more than the coals. She was drowning in it.

She turned to say something innocuous and the

words drifted with the smoke. He kissed her. Just like that, one hand lightly on her cheek and his mouth warm. The sensation of his kiss settled in her spine and the heat on her cheek was suddenly bone deep. She put her hands on either side of his face and let her own kiss linger over his mouth as if they were about to whisper to each other. No words, just soft pressure and the tip of his tongue finding hers. She never wanted to come up for air. "Goodness," she sighed.

"You're probably thinking I set this whole thing up," he murmured.

"You're making it tough to do much thinking."

"Who am I kidding tonight. Not you, green eyes."

"What thing did you set up?" She asked as she kissed him again, barely rubbing her lips over his.

"Kip and the baby-sitter."

She felt him inhale. "Did you?"

He kissed her again, holding her tighter. She needed the support. "This isn't why I accepted your dinner invitation, Shannon, but Lord, can you kiss."

She wasn't sure how to respond. "This isn't why I asked you to dinner."

"No. No, it was for puppet testing."

"Yes. My puppets." She stepped back and steadied her own breathing. He raked his hair as the moment hung between them. He gave her the uneasy feeling he was deep in some sort of internal wrestling match. She turned off the grill and lifted their dinner onto the platter. "I think maybe we should eat," she said.

He nodded. "That might be a good idea."

"And I think we should stick to small talk."

They sat at the small table in the evening light and suddenly he was all conversation. They talked about the city's Renaissance, the Andy Warhol Museum, the Steelers' last season and the current status of the Pirates. "How about those Bucs?" He said as they finished the wine.

She asked about the Head of the Ohio and he rambled on about other rowing competitions. Beyond her back garden fence children's voices rose and fell and the street noises filled in their silences. Bus brakes squealed occasionally. An evening freight train rolled in the distance. The intimacy finally grew comfortable again, as comfortable as the weight of his arm over her shoulder had been and as comfortably stimulating as the warmth of his mouth against hers.

They finished with coffee in the kitchen after bringing in their plates. He glanced at his watch. "I promised the sitter my last-minute request wouldn't interfere with her boyfriend's arrival at nine." He twirled the stem of his empty wineglass. "Feel like walking your date home?"

"Was this a date?"

He smiled. "Felt like one."

Dusk was settling in. This is comfortable, she thought as they walked in silence along the bend, deeper into Thurston Court. Lights were on, door lamps and upstairs bedrooms glowed. Mothers called children. A dog barked. "It can't be easy for you, staying here,'' she said as his town house came into view.

''As I said, it's easier for Kip.''

''May I ask how long you and Kate were married?''

They'd reached the driveway. He glanced at his watch again. ''Shannon, let me pay the sitter, then we'll talk. Will you stay? It's early.'' He snapped his fingers. ''Didn't I offer to bring the ice cream? Come on in for a dish. There's more to be said and I'm out of time.''

The enigma was offering to talk. It was too good to turn down. They were losing the light but there was enough to see what she hoped was sincerity in Nick's eyes before he turned and went in, leaving the door ajar. A moment later he appeared with a teenager who thanked him. ''Shannon McEvoy, Rachel Peters.'' They exchanged pleasantries as a sedan honked and pulled into the driveway next door. Rachel waved and hurried.

Shannon turned back to Nick. ''I'm sure you'll raise Kip to walk to the door and ring the bell.''

Nick laughed. ''Every male in every generation should have to suffer through the agony of making conversation with an anxious parent. One of the rites of passage.'' He ushered her into the foyer and turned, so close she could see the sweep of his thick lashes.

''Nick?''

He studied her and shook his head. He was wrestling again, she could sense it. One minute he was closer than the air they breathed, the next, gone to someplace she doubted she could reach. Instinct told her not to try. Not yet. Nick dug his hand through his thick hair again, then suddenly drew her into an embrace. No words. She moved into his arms, back into what was now familiar and kissed him as perfectly as she had at her house. He traced her lower lip with his tongue and she felt his fingers along the shell of her ears. She moved against him as he held her and tried to keep her head clear so she could decline what she sensed would come next.

She caught her breath. "Speaking of anxious fathers. Should we—or you—check on Kip? Maybe we should go upstairs."

His quiet laugh was rueful and he took her by the hand. "Maybe we should."

They climbed the stairs together and she stood at his shoulder as he opened the door. The dim glow from a night-light illuminated the top of a nursery dresser. She watched Nick's features soften as he stepped into the room. She was intruding on the intimacy and she stepped back into the door frame of the master bedroom to give him some privacy. Never in her life had she ached so badly to be kissed again, but not up here, not on the threshold of the bedroom. She hoped she looked worldly, not like the scared rabbit she felt.

"Dreamland. Completely tuckered out," he whispered as he came out and closed the door.

"Dreamland." She couldn't think of anything else to say and for a long moment she stood still, one foot on the carpeted bedroom floor, the other on the hardwood of the hall. She put her hands behind her to keep from reaching for him. His scrutiny made her turn away, toward the shadowed bed in a moment made awkward by the thundering of her pulse. She had to stifle the urge to press her ribs to get her heart to slow. She licked her bottom lip. He reached around and the heat of his fingers lingered a little too long over the base of her spine as he searched for her hand.

"Nick—"

"Follow me."

He tugged, not left into the bedroom, but right, across the hall and down the stairs, not just down the stairs but through the dining room and into the kitchen. He was silent until they were at the refrigerator. "Dutch Chocolate or French Kiss?" were the first words he said. He closed his eyes and pressed his head against the freezer door. "Damn. Would you believe me if I said I meant French Vanilla?"

It broke the ice. "Any reason why I shouldn't believe you?" She didn't wait for his answer. She laughed at his hapless expression. A flush had spread across his high cheekbones and she followed it with her finger. "Look at you."

"You have been."

"Yes, I guess I have."

"I've wanted to kiss you, Shannon McEvoy, since the moment Kip flipped out of your arms. When Evan opened the door Sunday night I thought you were a very married woman. Off-limits."

"But I turned out not to be a very married woman," she said, hardly above a whisper.

"You turned out to be every place I looked. The grocery store, the end of the block. My dinner partner."

This time his kiss was deep, searching, full of as much promise as restraint. His hands played and pressed over her back and down her spine to the spot he'd explored upstairs and she wondered if he could tell that it was still warm from his touch. They leaned into each other. She had a view of the refrigerator instead of the bed but it didn't feel any safer. He tensed. The hug tightened and he laughed deep into her hair. They kissed passionately, like teenagers on a front stoop or lovers in the back seat of a father's car. The heat of his touch moved up her spine to her neck, into her hair and back. He ran his fingers over the small of her back as if they were dancing, then slowly the pressure moved. He cupped her hips and held him to her.

"You make me forget," he said in her hair.

Forget Kate? The words dissolved as she lost herself in the pleasure of Nick Goulding's touch. Safer in the kitchen? She was jelly, syrup, molten lava and grateful they weren't still at the top of the stairs.

"Shannon." She was being gently moved to arm's length. "This is wonderful. You're wonderful, close to irresistible."

"I was under the impression we were going to have some conversation, maybe even ice cream. That's what I walked down here for."

"Did you?"

She cocked her head. "Nick, I hope you don't think—"

"Timing is everything," he was saying. "Damn, this is hard. I want what you want but I need space, Shannon. No distractions this week."

Her own cheeks flamed. "Nick, you're implying I've been chasing you. Dinner tonight—"

"Was meant for Kip and the puppets. I shouldn't have come down alone. You're ruining my concentration."

"That sounds like a compliment."

"Oh, brother, is it."

"I'm more of a distraction than working with a two-year-old around your ankles? What on earth could I have to do with any of your sociological papers?"

"Distraction. Concentration." He found her mouth. She licked her lips and made it easy, but kept her eyes wide-open as he pushed his fingers through her hair and tilted her head.

"Distance, remember, Nick?"

"You look right into my soul, Shannon."

"I haven't gotten nearly that deep. You leave a person with an armload of questions." She wound her arms comfortably around his neck and moved back into a perfect fit. When he finally released her, she took a deep breath and let it out slowly through pursed lips. "What makes you think I'm the least bit interested in more than conversation?"

"It might have something to do with the way you feel and the way you move and the way you make

me respond to all of it. Every living inch.'' He kept
right on looking until her flush was back. He ran his
tongue lightly over her lips and she opened her
mouth, until the kiss was deep and urgent and a promise. ''Right now I want to be upstairs in that bed as
much as you do, but, Shannon, my timing's off. I
need all your irresistibleness at arm's length for a
while. One of us needs a clear head and unfortunately
it looks like I'm the one.''

She missed half his soliloquy as she pulled back
against the butcher block countertop. ''Clear head,
wait one minute.''

He was still heavy-lidded. ''Don't misunderstand.
I wanted you upstairs as much as you wanted to be
there. The way you suggested we check on Kip and
glanced across that bed nearly unglued me.''

''You thought I was trying to get you into bed?''

He ran his thumb along her cheek and laughed.
''Shannon, don't be coy. It's not your style, thank
goodness. I love it, all of it, starting with the dinner
invitation for Kip.''

She smothered a pinprick of guilt and let the shock
of his words and their implications settle. At her full
height they were almost eye to eye. ''I wanted Kip to
try out puppets. I threw in dinner as thanks.'' She
grimaced at the humor in Nick's eyes. ''You I threw
in because you're a package deal. Kip's a little young
to walk down to my place by himself, not that he
hasn't done that already.''

''Package deal. I like that.'' He seemed to falter.

"I admit I was no candidate for Father of the Year on Sunday."

"You were a candidate for the department of child welfare. And, I might point out, tonight it was you who came up with some cockamamy story about how cranky Kip was, you who got a sitter and you who showed up on my doorstep with a bottle of wine instead of a two-year-old."

"Guilty as charged on that one."

"There. See?"

"What?"

She didn't know exactly what and waved her hand in the air. She only knew she hadn't finished. "You honestly think I agreed to walk home with you, not because you said you had more things to tell me, not because you had to get home to your baby-sitter, but because I wanted to get you under your ex-wife's sheets, in your ex-wife's bed, with your son in the next room?"

"Shannon, I meant it as a compliment. Believe me, I'm every bit as drawn to you. That's the problem— at the moment. I love the way you respond—"

"Respond is the operative word, Nick. You, all gorgeous and charming, have been giving off sparks like a Fourth of July sparkler. Of course I respond, but you've seemed to confuse those kisses with—" She was puffed up and embarrassed and words escaped her, which only built her anger. "Other stuff," she concluded.

"Other stuff."

"If I were ever to go to bed with you—which is

the furthest thing from my mind—it would be because I love you—which I don't—and because I want to continue an intimacy, which we started up here.'' She tapped his temple. ''Which we haven't, hard as I've tried. You take six steps backward for every one that goes forward.''

''I know. That's what I've been trying to discuss with you.''

''Discuss? This has been a night decidedly light on discussion. You've been trying a lot of stuff with me, Nick, and all of it has to do with my nerve endings. There have been damn few words thrown in.''

''Do I deserve all this just because I asked for a little time?''

''Believe me, you can have all the time in the world. Go do your research, or bring peace to the Middle East or get over your ex-wife. Whatever it is you need time for, Nick dear, you've got it. I wouldn't dream of interrupting.''

She stopped because she was breathless. He stayed stock-still under the glare of the kitchen lights with his eyes wide and his lips pursed looking for all the world as if he was trying not to laugh, which would have been the absolute last straw.

''Shannon, as soon as you take time to inhale, could you go back to the gorgeous and charming part?''

''The only thing I'm going back to is my own house. My own sheets on my own bed. Alone.''

''Would it help if I apologize for misconstruing

your—'' He paused as if he were searching for a word. ''Actions?''

''Reactions, Nick. I went upstairs to check on a sleeping child.''

''Shannon, I already apologized.''

''I'd have to be made of granite not to react to your touch. You've got every cell in my body on alert.'' It must have been the wine. She threw her arms around his neck and gave him a quick, hard kiss as though he were a departing soldier off to the front. ''Nicholas Goulding, when I want to make love to you, you won't have to misconstrue furtive glances into another woman's darkened bedroom. You'll know. Believe me, you'll know.''

4

He did know. That was the hell of it. He earned his entire living with words. His command of the language, his turn of a phrase had won him respect and awards and a darn good salary, and now some puppet designer with an art degree and soul-searing glances had left him speechless.

Smoke and mirrors: her whole erratic, meandering, rambling tirade. He knew words, he knew women and he knew passion when he felt it. Shannon McEvoy could sputter and protest all she wanted. Despite every overheated insult she'd thrown at him, that statuesque package of irresistibleness would have followed him into Kate's bed, into his arms, hell, into the Monongahela if he'd pressed her. He hadn't. He'd been the perfect gentleman, a prince. So much for chivalry.

He was exhausted, having tossed and turned—alone—half the night composing apologies, fantasizing about intimate reconciliations that would only land him another harangue—if not a slap—if she had any inkling of what he was up to for the half-baked article. He'd spent an hour at the laptop in the hopes that recording some of it might clear his head. No luck there, either, and just when he'd dropped off to sleep Kip was up and ready for the day.

He ached for his loft, his own bed and his riverfront routine, which brought him back to the core of the problem. He had work to do, real work. Shannon McEvoy might have gotten the old journalistic wheels turning, but she was nothing but a stick in the spokes now. That was all he had wanted to explain last night, that and some of the confusion about Kate and Kip. He wasn't about to tell her about the article, of course, but she had every right to know Kip was his nephew and Kate was his sister. Now, damn it, even the passion was tangled and confused. Truth wasn't something he could throw at her feet, not at this stage, not if he ever wanted to glimpse those feet again.

Yesterday he'd devoted hours to the quagmire he was sinking in. He'd paid a baby-sitter, planned it all out in advance, all to get Shannon alone, all to explain. He'd had every intention of loosening the knots he'd tied himself up in since Sunday and now those knots were tighter than ever. Hell, he should have let her think he was married. It would have solved everything.

Nick broke from his reverie, glanced at his watch and eased Kip around a patio table on the sidewalk across from Time Out. Wednesday morning was warm and clear and Walnut Street was already bustling with vacationing students, fashionable East End matrons and the usual smattering of kids who insisted on skirting the street traffic on in-line skates, skateboards or mountain bikes. Not one of them looked bleary-eyed or punch-drunk. He yawned.

No research here. Humble pie was all he had on his mind, that and trying to decipher the minds of women. Shannon had wanted to try out puppets and, by God, she was about to get the chance. As soon as he kept his obligation he'd be off, toddler-in-tow, to the sprawling, anonymous suburban malls. He glanced at his watch. He could make Monroeville by late morning and cranky or not, Kip could skip his nap so they could scout Ross Park for part of the afternoon. Wednesday already and the assignment was due by the weekend. He was no better than a college freshman who'd put off a term paper till that last forty-eight hours. Today he'd get cracking. They could both hit the hay right after dinner.

He needed fresh turf. The environs of the city were proving treacherous. It wasn't just Shannon in the grocery store. The zoo, the grocery store and Schenley Park's playgrounds were far less of a hike than suburban malls, but he'd already had to dodge a neighbor and a fellow rower. He needed to play bachelor father in less familiar territory.

He checked his watch again. Ten a.m. The maroon door of Shannon's shop opened and she stepped into the sunlight. She held the door with her foot pressed on the brass kick-plate and set a straight-back chair against the brick exterior. Her loose-fitting dress caught the breeze and lay against those long, fabulous legs as she turned. It was a bandanna print or paisley or something else not much weightier than handkerchief fabric layered over a small, body-fitting T-shirt. She looked rested, positively refreshed. Her hair was up again, that shiny pile of copper he'd run his fingers through last night while she'd kissed the life out of him. Or into him, he thought with a sudden, welcome heat.

"Ow. You're hurting." Kip yanked his fingers from Nick's grasp.

Nick ruffled Kip's shaggy hair. "Sorry, buddy. Sometimes a woman makes you hang on for dear life. Our friend Shannon is across the street."

She went into the store and reappeared with an enormous teddy bear that she propped in the chair, then adjusted an Open sign under his chin. A shaft of sunlight caught her and she raised her hand against it, then went back inside. Nick walked with Kip at his knees and watched her disappear. He smacked into the edge of a table. "Sorry," he muttered to the coffee drinkers as their mugs jiggled and they adjusted their sunglasses. "Sorry."

"Mine." Kip grabbed a half-eaten croissant from the table.

"Yours," Nick replied to the still-startled coffee drinker as he put it back on the plate with an ingratiating smile. At the curb he knelt to his nephew and pointed across the street. "See the bear by the red door? We're going into the store so you can try out some puppets. You're going to like this adventure a whole lot more than I will. Hold tight while we cross."

Kip cheered and darted from his grasp. He had one

small leg already suspended over the curb as Nick scooped him over his hip. "Oh, no, you don't. The only safe way to get you across is to stuff you in my pocket." Kip squirmed and laughed and yelped as Nick aimed him at the far side of the street. "We're heading for that bear, kiddo, but we've got to get there legally."

He walked farther along the block to the stop sign and crosswalk at the corner. No doubt the ever-cautious Kate had already started her son on jaywalking lectures. Today marked the halfway point of the baby-sitting adventure and he already had all the proof he needed that there was a darn sight more he required in the way of parenting skills.

"Bear!"

"Yup. We're going to visit the bear. It's Shannon's bear."

"Shannon's bear."

By the time Nick reached the other side of the street, Kip was still propped horizontally in his arms with his small hands out in front of him like Superman. Nick continued to steer him past smiling window-shoppers. Most, he'd already noted, were women. "Bear lover coming through," Nick said.

Half a dozen admiring female glances went from Kip right up to meet him head-on. He could practically see them spinning their own fantasies. Maybe he'd try the rocket approach at the mall. He was twenty feet from the bear in a blur of passersby when one of the women stopped.

"Nick?" he heard from behind him.

He turned to the brunette who had just stepped aside to let them pass. Karen Holland. He recognized her face, remembered the wild, naturally curly hair pulled back in barrettes at her temples. He glanced at her earrings—handcrafted, small bits of brass.

She smiled. He glanced guiltily at Kip while she shifted a designer shopping bag and the skinniest loaf of French bread he'd ever seen. "Nick. Nick Hansen." She went up on tiptoe and gave him a kiss on the cheek.

He tucked Kip under his left arm and added a handshake, then set the toddler on his feet and went down on one knee mumbling instructions to Kip.

She knelt next to him. "It's been a while but surely you haven't forgotten. Karen. Karen Holland. Freelancer. We met at the journalism conference. When I found out you were a rower I talked you into a tour of the boathouse storage bays to look at the rowing shells that miserably cold February a few years back. Parlayed it into the feature article on Pittsburgh's crew teams. I sold it to *Rowing* magazine. Remember? We also talked about the piece I wrote on Haiti." She wiggled her multiringed left hand and smiled.

Of course he remembered. It was Karen Holland who had originally made the observation that single women were suckers for bachelor fathers.

"Karen Holland. Later we got into the discussion on women and their rings."

"Which you promised to turn into a Jake O'Donnell classic."

"I did."

She pouted. "The ring discussion was much later in the evening, I recall, upstairs in front of that roaring fire you built in the boathouse club room. I had to read your column in the *Register*. I at least deserved a signed draft."

Nick raised both hands in supplication. "You disappeared. I swear I tried to call you the next week."

"Malawi. Remember? I was off to Africa. Human interest stuff for a Peace Corps article. I suppose I did make vague promises that I'd call when I got back."

"And you didn't," he added, somewhat relieved to be able to shift the blame.

She glanced at Kip. "I should have. Anyway, here I am."

He made a point of looking at her hand. "Wearing more rings than ever."

She laughed again and fished through her purse, finally handing him a business card. "Engaged actually. Will Stevens, one of those Pittsburgh Peace Corps doctors I went over to interview."

"No kidding. There's a feature story in there somewhere."

"Don't you go and write it. This one's all mine." She looked back down at Kip. "Speaking of feature stories." She knelt again. "Who might you be?"

"Kip."

"Do you belong to this famous journalist?"

Nick shifted as Kip buried his face against his leg then looked up at him. "Time for the bear. You promised, Tendaddy." He repeated and pointed.

Karen stood. ''This darling child is yours? Ten-daddy?''

''In a manner of speaking.''

''I stayed too long in Africa.''

''It takes some explaining.''

''Am I jumping to conclusions?''

''A few.'' Lord, he felt like a teenager caught out after curfew.

''I never pinned you as the marrying kind. Or a dad, to boot.'' She looked bemused. ''Do I know her?''

''Her?''

''Is there a wife?'' She pulled his left hand into hers and looked at his fingers. ''No band. Not that an empty ring finger means anything, as Jake O'Donnell has already pointed out.''

''No wife.'' He got a raised eyebrow in response. ''It's a long story. I borrowed him for a sociological experiment I'm researching—kids and their toys.''

''Or would that be single women and bachelor dads? Nick Hansen, don't tell me I've inspired another Jake O'Donnell column.''

Kip was pulling at him. ''Now,'' turned into a whine.

Karen laughed. ''Get a sitter some night and have dinner with Will and me. Fill us in.'' She shifted the French bread. ''Am I allowed to ask who Kip's mother is?''

''Kate. Kate Goulding.'' Darned if he didn't stumble over the truth as badly as he stumbled over the lies.

* * *

Nick steered Kip toward Time Out with his already overtaxed brain reeling. Karen Holland of all people in all places. He entered the store with his fist pressed against the knot in his stomach.

Shannon was there, of course, behind the counter, as engrossed in her work as he was in her. The small shop was already bustling with customers. Puppets sat on the shelves behind her and marionettes hung from their strings from a sort of mobile hung in the rafters. Kip craned his neck. Across the room in a more protected area there was a dollhouse, and behind glass counters, miniature furniture of every description. Intricate reproductions. Superb craftsmanship. He tried not to think about how precise and delicate her touch must be. The only things safely within reach were stuffed animals piled in wicker baskets.

"Bears!"

Shannon raised her head. Her look of surprise and frank delight set his heart back to racing. The delight, of course, was no more than a flash that disappeared as she came from around the counter.

"Hello, Nick. This is quite a surprise."

He tried his best to look right into her deep green skepticism. "Shannon."

She knelt. "Hey, buddy." Back on her feet she did her best to stay solemn. "I didn't expect to see you."

"I'm making up for my substitution last night. I brought Beaujolais to dinner instead of the two-year-old, remember?" She flushed fast and furiously. Good, she remembers plenty, he thought, but his good intentions evaporated. He would have kissed her on the spot if he'd thought for a moment he could get away with it. "I believe you have some puppets waiting?" he said instead.

"I just want to repeat," she whispered as she took a step closer, "I would never use an innocent child to my own advantage." She took a step back. "Things are pretty busy." She turned to her assistant and began introductions. "Meg Bazley, these are the Gouldings, Nick and his son, Kip." Son. One of the many misunderstandings he had intended to clear up by now. His ears burned. "We'll be in the back for a few minutes. Come get me if things get too backed up."

"Shannon," he tried.

"Follow us," she replied over her shoulder as she turned and took Kip by the hand.

Anywhere.

Shannon led them into a back room almost as large as the front, partitioned for storage, a small desk for operations and an area set aside for what he presumed were her classes. There were bins of bits of fabric, beads, craft items he couldn't begin to name and a drying area where papier-mâché puppet heads were propped on dowel rods.

"Puppet, miniatures and doll-making workshops," she said, then promptly turned her attention to Kip. "Down here, sweetie." She was practically cooing as she settled him on the rug. She stood and stretched for a box. He should have offered, but Shannon McEvoy on tiptoe, arms extended, tugged every muscle in his own body. He rocked back on his heels and stayed where he was.

With the box in hand, she joined Kip on the floor and opened the lid slowly to reveal a pile of shapeless hand puppets. Nick watched as she laid out creatures similar to the ones he'd seen at dinner the night before.

Shannon was giving Kip her full attention, absently patting his hair, leaning close to decipher his toddler vocabulary, laughing at his growls and giggles. Nick shoved his hands into his khakis and rocked back on his heels, ignored and invisible. The maternal instinct in high gear, he thought, sorry he didn't dare pull out his notebook and pencil.

His cynical journalistic pulse began to pound. This could all be a colossal act to get his attention. Puppets as the ploy might have backfired last night, but here they were, after all, at her store. One way or another she'd landed the guy in the shop, secreted away in the back room. A few purposeful moments with the kid would be enough to melt a man's heart. He stayed still waiting for a meaningful glance, another one of her breath-catching flushes, the flutter of an eyelid. Nothing.

He watched, mesmerized by her patience, the timbre of her voice and the grace of her hands as she unwrapped the puppets. He stood in the corner, an intruder, as she offered the selection to Kip and let him pick his own. "Now up inside," she said quietly. "I don't want to help. Can you get your fingers to make the eyes blink? Tell me if they reach."

Nick watched his nephew laugh. "They reach," he shrieked as he made a kangaroo lower its fantastically long eyelashes. He tried a puppy. Its little mouth opened in time to Kip's growl. A moment later he had a monkey clapping. There were larger ones too big for his small hands and some too sophisticated for his two-year-old motor skills. Shannon scribbled notes on the box. Suddenly she turned and glanced over at Kip, obviously aware of his scrutiny. A smile started in her eyes and lighted her face. Briefly. She turned back and ran a tape measure along Kip's fingers and then his arm.

"Tickles," he giggled.

Gooseflesh ran under Nick's shirt.

Kip measured Shannon's arm, too, and dissolved into more laughter when she put a rabbit on her hand and made it kiss his cheek. Nick's cheek tingled. His mouth went dry.

Meg appeared at the door. "The light kits and doll-house lamps have finally arrived."

"At last. Would you call the woman from Point Breeze and tell her they're in? I'll come out shortly. Kip and I are almost finished."

Kip and I. Nick jingled the loose change deep in his pockets. Shannon was on her feet. "Thank you for bringing Kip over, Nick. I wish I could have given him more time." She touched his arm, then pulled back as if she'd broken some resolution.

"Almost forgot you were angry with me?"

"I haven't forgotten anything."

Fire and ice, he thought, as he jammed his hands

back into his pockets. He wished he were giving her the impression of total nonchalance. As if that were remotely possible.

She turned back to Kip and pulled the kangaroo from the box. "Would you like to keep him? You did such a good job with the eyes."

"Whiffley nose," he replied with more giggles.

She smiled. "Whiffley nose."

"Let me pay for it," Nick tried.

"Of course not. It's a thank-you for his help." Kip scooted past them and into the shop, stopping in front of the display of stuffed animals. They were alone and for the moment, out of sight.

"Shannon?" Nick touched her arm with no resolution except to keep his hand on her warm, dry skin. He was close enough to watch her breath catch, close enough to inhale a hint of scent, something light, intoxicating, close enough to feel her cool green gaze heat his skin. He looked again at Kip, safe at the basket, then stepped from view.

He touched her cheek, watched her wide-eyed glance grow solemn while he searched for words. None came. Instead his heart thundered in amazement as she raised her hands and slid them along his temples. He hardly dared close his eyes against surprise of the cool touch that raised such heat. Without a word she pressed her mouth against his, warm, closed, soft. She was kissing him. He felt her against him, tall and straight and perfect. He muffled the moan that caught in his throat while they kissed. Incredible.

He ached to be anywhere but where they were. He

ached to be alone with her. He just plain ached, long after the kiss. She let him brush her shoulders and he dared slide his fingers over the scoop neck of her T-shirt. "Great hair," he whispered as if stolen passion in the back room was what they had both intended all along. "Great copper hair and those wide Irish eyes. The only thing missing are the freckles."

"I have some."

"How could I have missed them?"

"Because they are dabbled over places you're not likely to see any time soon."

"Lord, Shannon."

"I have customers waiting."

"I know. Look, will you take that kiss as an apology? Last night got way out of hand. We said things—"

"Apology accepted."

He blinked. "Just like that?"

She stepped aside, away from the door. "I was hoping you'd come to your senses and apologize. Not another problem?"

He tried to joke. "We're supposed to discuss—things. You're supposed to insist it was partly your fault, you know, rehash—things—ask for a fresh start. Or I could ask for one."

"I wouldn't dream of asking for a fresh start. You want space. Have you forgotten? I haven't. I do owe you an apology, though, and here it is—I never should have let things go as far as they did, not under these circumstances. You asked for distance, Nick, which you obviously, desperately need. I'm in complete agreement. Go."

"Go? Ten seconds ago you were standing in my arms kissing me into the day after tomorrow."

She stepped back. "You were doing the kissing. I was doing the enjoying. There's no denying you're a master in the physical department. I just wanted a little reminder before you go get your space. Great way to get my day started."

"You were using me?" He groaned at the ridiculousness of his comment.

"To be perfectly honest, Nick, I did a lot of thinking last night when I got home. I even thought about calling, but of course I had no way to look up the number since I don't know what Kate's married name is now. Walking back down the street for any more chitchat seemed inappropriate." She glanced out into the store.

"Thinking about what?"

She glanced into the showroom. "Never mind. We have a hard and fast rule about leaving children unattended. Says so right at the counter. Thank you for bringing Kip in this morning. You'd better get back to him."

She left him. Just like that. As if nothing had transpired but the foolish puppet testing, warm, flushed Shannon McEvoy exacted revenge by once again igniting everything he'd been determined to douse. She left him leaning against the storage room wall with blood coursing through parts better left ignored. He stared at the marionettes hung up to dry. "I know just how you feel," he muttered.

Damn right he needed breathing room. Forget chivalry. Forget puppet design. Forget Shannon McEvoy. Rewrite the article without a mention of her. He could find another opening, a better hook than his toddler's back flips into her geraniums. He could concoct something better than a lost shoe in the produce aisle and a trumped-up invitation to dinner. If he knew what was good for him—hadn't he always—he could live without her for the next few days. Those great legs, that dazzling smile could wait.

Shannon McEvoy wasn't supposed to be part of any of this. A simple brainstorm of an idea had been complicated by raging hormones, his and hers. Simple observation of the feminine response to a single man with a child in tow. Cute. Clever. Damned clever. None of this was supposed to be complicated. His personal life had always been separate from his journalistic endeavors. Always had been no matter how squirrelly his notions and offbeat the themes of his columns. Didn't he know better than most that hell hath no fury... He sucked in a breath and waited for his pulse to slow and his blood to cool. There was no way, however, that he was going to clear his head until he was miles—planets—from the woman scorned who was already deliberately busy with another customer. All he wanted was the last word and he'd be gone; Kip with him.

Once out of the storage room he made a beeline

for the stuffed animals as Kip pulled a small bear from the basket. Nick knelt. "Let's take him home."

"Okay!"

He waited until Meg was busy with a customer. "Give it to Shannon at the cash register," he added as he lifted his nephew and crossed the store. Kip dropped the teddy bear on the counter.

Shannon smiled at Kip. "You're sure?"

"Sure!"

"Does he have a name yet?"

Kip leaned shyly back into Nick's neck. "Kisses."

Nick could have sworn Shannon blanched. "Kisses?" She handed the bear back.

"I'll give him lots." This time Nick flushed as Kip suddenly nuzzled the bear against his neck.

"Fifteen dollars, plus tax. Cash, check or credit card?"

He set Kip back on his feet and reached for his wallet. "Plastic." He pulled out the credit card. His mood worsened. *Nicholas Hansen* jumped at him from its gold embossing. He shoved the card back into his wallet, in front of the *Nicholas Hansen* Pennsylvania driver's license and the *Nicholas Hansen* auto club card. Guilt, panic and cold sweat made him suck in a sharp breath. Credit card. How could he have been so stupid? He prayed he wouldn't have to come up with some lame excuse for running outside to an ATM machine as he rifled his billfold. "Changed my mind. There you go," he said finally as he laid enough bills on the counter.

"Cash. You're a rare man." It was barely a murmur.

Rare. He was feeling closer to well-done, completely cooked.

"Do you think Kate would like to be on our mailing list?" she added.

"Kate?"

Shannon slid a guest book across the counter. "Your old Kate. Ex-Kate." She let out a breath. "Exwife. This is our mailing list. Private, of course. Under no circumstances do we sell customers' names to anyone else. It entitles her to discounts, classes, that sort of thing. Free puppet shows for the kids." She picked up the pen. "I didn't recognize her from her photographs and since I don't think I've seen Kip before Sunday, I'm presuming she's not a frequent visitor to the shop. If you'll tell me her married name, I'll check the computer when I get a minute. If she's not on our list, I'll add her."

It was the second time she'd asked for the surname. "Goulding." It came out before he could think. Even with a counter between them, proximity to Shannon McEvoy made him feel as if she was sanding him off around the edges, dulling what was left of the wits he lived by while desire simmered worse than a Miami Beach sunburn.

She looked puzzled. "Goulding? She still uses your name?"

He fumbled, tried to put on a tragic expression. Anything. This was not the time to confess to yet another distortion of the truth. "No, of course not. I forget sometimes."

"Exactly how long has it been since you two split up?"

"Recent. This is all still new," he added, delighted to see a flash of something besides disdain in her eyes. Sympathy? Empathy? She actually winced. He felt better already. "I guess I'm still raw." He pushed the book back to her. "What I mean is, this is something I shouldn't get involved in—her new life—making these kinds of decisions for her. Not anymore."

"Of course not. I shouldn't have suggested it. I was a fool not to see, not to understand your real situation."

"Real situation?"

He watched her nod at him in mute, sympathetic, total misunderstanding. "Oh, Nick, I apologize. You're such a lousy liar. It isn't some academic research is it? That hasn't made sense. I've thought maybe you're in the CIA or an undercover cop or something. I should have recognized the reason why you want space, time." She waved at the air with a flush creeping from her T-shirt.

She thinks I need distance because of Kate, he realized. Lightning, he was convinced, would strike him dead before the day was over. He leaned forward. "Shannon, there were things I meant to discuss last night."

She stiffened. "No, no, I apologize. I didn't realize what you've been trying to tell me. It's all right, Nick. You've finally spoken from your heart. Just spare me the guilt-ridden expression. No grief, either. Surely you must understand that I'm really not interested in stories about ex-wives men haven't gotten over. Not yours or anybody else's. I suspected it all along, of course. I see what you're grappling with. Something far closer to the bone than research and all the rest I teased you about.''

The knots around his heart tightened as she turned to indicate there were others to be waited on. ''Customers, Nick. Sorry. Call me sometime in the future if you'd like, but make it after you're finished grappling.''

5

"Call me if you like," Nick muttered for the hundredth time as he pushed Kip and the stroller through the mall and tried to pay attention to appreciative glances and appraisals half an hour later. "Easy for you to grin," he said as Kip arched his neck and looked up at him. "A puppet in one arm and a teddy bear in the other."

"Kisses."

"I know all about kisses. That's what got me into this mess."

"Kisses." The name turned to a wail as Kip struggled to get out of the stroller. When Nick finally looked down at him he realized the bear was missing.

Nick groaned and turned the stroller around as he searched the path they'd just forged through the bustling shoppers. "Kisses," Kip began to shriek.

He bent and wiped Kip's tears with his sleeve. "Hold on, little guy."

"This must be yours." The voice was at his ear and he rocked back on his haunches. "Or yours," a brunette continued as she put Kisses into Kip's outstretched arms. The woman was kneeling two inches from him. "If you aren't the cutest thing," she was murmuring.

She wasn't so bad herself. Where was his enthusiasm? Nick tried to drum up something besides indifference as she stood and began introductions. There were coy remarks and he could have sworn at least two furtive glances at his ring finger. Open that mental notebook, he told himself. Pay attention.

"Katherine," she was saying. "Kate, to my friends."

His mind wandered. How could Shannon misconstrue a little stumbling over the mention of Kate? He shook hands and managed to come up with, "Nicholas Goulding." What had possessed him to try to joke with a word like *raw*. *Raw*. He winced.

"You said raw?"

Nick blinked and apologized and made inane small talk about nap time.

"Afternoons can be a killer. I have a three-year-old, myself," she was saying. "Since his father and I split up I've gone through three nannies."

He failed to see the correlation but managed to keep a limp conversation going as they moved toward the food court. When she nodded at a dress shop and excused herself, he waved weakly and kept going. Some sociologist he was.

"Call me if you like," he muttered, still quoting Shannon. She'd set him on the stove to boil then chewed him into little pieces. He shook his head to clear it and found a bench. Kip was still clinging to Kisses as a woman took the space next to them.

"Adorable," she said.

"Kisses," Kip replied shyly.

He hated the word. Kissing Shannon McEvoy had made every fiber in his overworked body hum. Parts of him were still humming as he tried to focus on the newest research opportunity sharing the bench with him. All he could think about was the Time Out storage room. He and Shannon could have put the place into spontaneous combustion. Instead the web of deception he was weaving was quickly unraveling.

At 7:00 p.m., Shannon pulled the last packages of glue sticks out of the packing box and set them on her desk in the room she was transforming into a combination studio and home office. She'd changed into jeans and an oversize cast-off polo shirt of Evan's, determined to put in a full evening of setting the town house to rights. If it were only as easy to put herself in order.

Evan had helped set up shelves along one wall. Tonight she'd lay out the wicker and wooden bins and get her craft supplies organized. She pressed her breastbone where the Chinese takeout dinner was talking back and chewed a couple of antacid tablets instead of simply sitting down and letting her dinner digest. Her entire day had been indigestion-inducing.

Letting Nick Goulding kiss the daylights out of her in the back room had not been the way she'd intended to start it. What had possessed her to get so forward? She raked her hair and shoved it from her eyes. Lord, she was even adopting his gestures.

It had been a day of revelations and from the moment he and Kip had left the shop she'd fought her misery. Nick was still in pain—if not in love—over his ex-wife. Hadn't there been enough hints? She berated herself for not figuring it out in front of the cereal aisle or over dinner or during the walk down to his town house—make that Kate's town house. Remarried and Kip barely two. Had she had a secret lover all along? How tough on the child. How horrible for Nick. Had he tried for a reconciliation? Had he thought of custody?

Nick Goulding was a puzzle and putting the pieces together when there'd been at least three feet of cool air between them might have saved her from the carrying on by her grill, kissing him at Kate's, not to mention that very morning in her storage room.

What had possessed her? She pressed her ribs again as the chalky antacids began to work. Why on earth had it taken her so long to comprehend? The hedging, his elusive answers should have told her immediately that this was a man not nearly as carefree as he pretended. She ached from more than indigestion when she thought of how lost he'd been in the diaper and baby food aisles of the grocery store, no doubt Kate's domain.

Kate had probably shopped for Kip's diapers and food and having to find his son's supplies on his own was just one more painful reminder of his new status. How new, she still wanted to know and grimaced at the recollection of his choice of words. "Raw," he'd said and raw was exactly how she felt.

She'd thought about little else the whole day and she still cringed. How blithely smug she'd been as she ordered him to grapple with his emotions. Nick was a man in pain and she should have picked up on it the minute she saw his behavior in Kate's house.

All week she'd been too involved in the turmoil of her own emotions to see what was really behind his actions. She shoved her loose hair out of her eyes again and got back to unpacking. Okay, suggesting puppet testing on Kip had been a ploy to get Nick to come to dinner. Okay, so he'd seen right through it. She tried to ignore the pang of embarrassment.

She glanced from the window to the closet. Her second-floor office was the equivalent of Kip's bedroom. The realization annoyed her. His small chest of drawers with the night-light sat by the window where her desk was. If he had shelves they were, no doubt, full of stuffed animals and picture books. Kisses the bear probably sat on one right now. Or maybe Kip was already snuggled up with it in his crib. She glanced to the right where his bed would be. Nick and Kate had probably picked out their son's furniture together, or maybe the nursery set had been one of theirs, handed down. A lump reformed in her throat, the same one that had kept her on the brink of tears most of the afternoon. Grapple, she'd thrown at him, even after he'd uttered *raw*. He was grappling already; she could see it now and her cavalier attitude had only made it worse.

She blinked as she realized she'd been standing in the middle of the room. With an oath under her breath, she got back to the task at hand and yanked a newspaper-wrapped lump from an open box. A Jake O'Donnell column peeked at her from the left of the crumpled newsprint.

Speak Up And Give A Guy A Break
Darlin', It's Your Mind We're After

Shannon smirked at the cigar-chomping photo of the columnist and the usual ire-provoking headline.

"How does an old guy who looks like a prize-fighter on a bad day get the gall to think he's an authority on men's attitudes about women?" she said to no one as she balled the newspaper and tossed it in the direction of the trash. "What about a guy's mind, Mr. O'Donnell?" she said to the mess. "That's what we're after. Why can't a guy just lay his cards on the table, instead of tiptoeing around every issue, skirting questions and sending up smoke screens. Do you have an answer for that, Jake?"

She muttered while she worked and after twenty minutes of bending, sank cross-legged to the floor to give her back a rest. She glanced back at the newspaper while she massaged her spine. "It's the nineties," Jake's column read.

You want my opinion? Keep coyness locked up with the Elvis records. Working up some master plan? Forget it. A guy could use a fresh approach now and then. You want to take me to dinner? Take me to dinner! Just do me and the rest of

the male population a favor—come right out and
ask. Hey, I'll even spring for the tip if there's no
pussyfooting around, no dropping whispery hints
I'm just as likely to miss. Thanks just the same.
Think like a man. It'll get you one every time.

"Think like a man," Shannon muttered, but as she
got back on her feet, she gave the newspaper page
another glance. Why hadn't she just been honest and
asked Nick to dinner? She should have suggested a
sitter for Kip instead of concocting the silly puppet
plan that she'd been hotly denying ever since, denying while accusing Nick of the same thing. How, she
asked herself, had things gotten so convoluted?

"Thanks just the same, Jake, but it'll be a cold day
on the Allegheny before I ask any male to dinner
again," she said out loud as she placed the last of her
balsa wood strips into the dollhouse bin.

Heat suddenly pressed the back of her throat; her
vision blurred. Tears, as unexpected as Jake
O'Donnell's column, threatened to squeeze their way
through her lashes. What the heck was this? She
couldn't even name the cause. Regret? Remorse? Empathy? She kicked at the discarded newspaper. She'd
played a good game that morning, all flip and confident. Now she gritted her teeth and swore. No man
had ever wound her up like this, spring-tight, ready
to snap.

She ached to set things right. Jake O'Donnell was
off by a mile. *Keep coyness locked up with the Elvis
records...no hints I'm likely to miss.* She pressed her

eyes with her sleeve. Men like Nick Goulding couldn't handle honesty. Men like Nick didn't want honesty. They wanted a few pleasant moments between the closest set of sheets, even if they belonged to an ex-wife.

Being flip with offhand remarks was one thing. If she got all sincere and told Nick she'd be interested *after* he had time to heal, *after* he came to terms with his loss, he'd hit the sidewalk running, Kip with him. She emptied three packing boxes and laid the shelves with more wicker baskets, ceramic mugs of pens, pencils and brushes, bits of fabric and coordinated ribbons until the room was worthy of a house magazine layout. It did nothing for the ache.

Think like a man. It'll get you one every time. Jake O'Donnell's words ran through her head like too-familiar lyrics of a popular song. She wasn't after Nick, not any longer, not with his life so upside down. She swore. He just needed to understand that she hadn't meant to be flip or cruel. She snorted at the column. She needed to apologize, apologize and protect her own heart. For the third time that day she wished she knew Kate's new surname so she could call him and do it over the phone.

By the time she left her town house it was eight forty-five, the same soft shadowy light the night she'd walked Nick home. Last night. Twenty-four hours. Anxiety tightened her muscles. She forced herself forward before she chickened out, rehearsing a lame-brain opening for when he opened his front door. Kate's front door.

At the turn in the bend a woman was watering her flowerpots and waved. "Welcome to the neighborhood," she called. "I've seen you gardening," she continued as she walked to the curb, "and had every intention of coming up to say hello. I'm Amy Lawson."

"Shannon McEvoy. Just as well you haven't come by. I've been too busy to stop and chat."

They continued with small talk that eased Shannon's tension, until she realized they were losing the light. "Do come by, now that I'm a little more settled. Anytime. Or the shop," she added, after discovering that Amy had young children. She glanced up the street. "I'm on my way up to the Goulding town house. No." She shook her head. "That's his name. Anyway I'm going right up around the bend on Winchester Place."

Amy followed her glance. "There is a Goulding family up there. Kate and Paul."

"Excuse me?"

"The Gouldings. They have a little boy, Nicholas. Paul's with one of the colleges, Chatham, I think."

She felt herself blanch. "Would he be in the sociology department? You're sure his name is Goulding?"

"Paul? I don't know what he teaches, but that's his name. Tallish. Quite good-looking... I'm sorry, Shannon. I seem to have confused you."

She looked up the lane. "No, Amy, you're not the one confusing me."

She forced herself forward, which took nearly as much effort as forcing back the hot, ripping sensation at the back of her throat. Frustration balled her fists. She was locked in a mental maze and every time she turned a corner, there was nothing ahead but more tunnels. Now would be the perfect time to turn on her heel and retreat to the safety of her disheveled condominium except that she was not about to retreat, not until she had answers; not until she had a clear head and a clear conscience. She forced herself forward to the loop that became Winchester Place. Dusk was pulling color from his house. The dark green shutters looked black. She stood at the curb. Married. Paul Goulding. What kind of self-serving, womanizing...

Light pooled on the grass at the edge of the walled patio. She forced herself up the front walk as far as the exterior opening to the courtyard wall. Fingers of light cascaded onto the patio from the open French doors. Unseen from the road, Nick sat at the dining-room table under the glare of the overhead chandelier. He had on a navy blue T-shirt and he was hammering away at a laptop computer while he glanced occasionally at a small open notebook.

"Research," she muttered. She should have gone to the front door and rung the bell, but there wasn't enough gumption left in her to make it that far. Instead she summoned her last scraps of courage and propelled herself forward onto the patio. She knocked on the open French door. The sliding screen was locked. Nick stood up so fast his chair fell over backward. It was then she realized he had nothing else on but boxer shorts.

"Shannon? What the heck are you doing out there? I never— This is—" He picked up the overturned chair.

The boxers were a green tartan plaid. Black Watch absurdly popped into her head. "Put some pants on. We need to talk," she replied.

"Talk? This morning you said you didn't want to hear from me." He followed her glance. "I was on my way to bed, as soon as I got some work done. I wanted to get through some notes I took today...hard with Kip. Of course nothing much can be done till he's asleep. I'm desperate for a decent night's rest myself." He looked over his shoulder and raked his hair. "Go to the front door while I grab my jeans. I'll let you in."

The sudden concern for modesty bolstered her confidence. She went back out to the walk and up to the front stoop. Nick opened the door zipping up his fly. There were a million comments she could have made as she looked at him, a million she expected to hear from him. His face was pure expectation; she could tell because she never took her eyes from his, afraid if she did, her glance would fall again to the rim of tartan elastic waistband rimming his hips just above the denim.

He didn't blush, he just finished with his zipper. She muttered an apology. She waited. An ambulance siren wailed in the distance, much too far away to inhibit any conversation. ''Not that I give a flying fig, but are you Paul Goulding?'' It made her throat burn to ask.

''Paul?'' His complexion darkened into a full-scale blush that clouded his eyes and swept across his cheeks into his ears. With the exception of her erratically thundering pulse, everything inside turned to stone. She had to give him credit, he managed to maintain eye contact. ''Has someone confused me with Kate's husband?''

''I know precious little about you, but one thing is clear. You're the color of a radish and a rotten liar.''

''I'm not Paul Goulding.''

''I was on my way down here and I ran into your neighbor. Out of innocent welcome to the neighborhood conversation, I find out that Kate's husband's last name is Goulding. Unless she married brothers, you owe me an explanation.'' She straightened. ''You owe me an explanation regardless.''

He stepped sideways. ''I think you'd better come in.''

''No, Nick, I think I'd better stay right where I am. I've been far too close, far too many times. I've had you in the CIA. I've had you doing undercover police work. Anything to keep from thinking you might be cheating on a wife and baby, cheating with me.''

''Shannon, you and I haven't done anything to be ashamed of.''

''Don't you dare suggest it isn't cheating because

we haven't rolled around under somebody's sheets. What you've already done with me is despicable.''

He sighed and leaned back against the open door he'd just tried to usher her through. ''What I've already done with you has totally upset my life, but it's not what you think.''

''What I think? Who can think around you? Who can follow for one crummy encounter your train of thought?''

''To tell you the truth, I've been having a hard time myself.''

Alarm stiffened her spine. ''You wouldn't know the truth if it jumped off the cereal shelf and into your shopping cart. When—exactly—have you ever told the truth?''

''Not lately.''

She bit her lip hard and it hurt, but it kept her from the humiliation of tears and a tirade she knew would wake Kip. ''At last.''

''Half the time I can't remember what the hell I've told you. Shannon McEvoy, you've got me so distracted and confused.''

The sudden confession deepened her pain. ''This is exactly what I mean. Don't you dare turn the conversation around and blame me. It's you, Nick or Paul or whoever-you-are Goulding, we were talking about. You.''

''Come inside.''

''It wouldn't be wise.'' She pointed past him. ''Besides, the last time I was down here, I took one look at those photos and you couldn't get me out of here fast enough.''

He grinned.

''Don't you dare smile at me.''

''If ever there were anyone who made me want to smile, it's you, Green Eyes.''

''Cut the bull. I don't know what kind of game you're playing, but I want some truth out of you. I think I deserve that much.''

He continued to smile. ''You have had some truth out of me. That's what's gotten me into this mess.''

''There. You agree it's a mess.''

''Worst I've ever been in.''

''And you've been in plenty, I suspect.''

He pressed his hand to his heart. ''I am not Paul Goulding. I am not Kate's husband. Shannon—''

''Don't Shannon me. I'm furious.'' She had to remind herself as he smiled because he was so close she could see the sun-lightened tips of his thick lashes and the steady throbbing of his pulse along his temple. ''Smug. Look at you.''

He shook his head. ''It's you I want to look at. Gorgeous. Every inch.''

''Don't be ridiculous. I'm standing here in Evan's old shirt and filthy jeans.''

''All fired up, wanting my head on a plate. Makes you glow, Shannon.''

''The only glowing I'm doing is from fury, Nick.''

She pointed her finger in warning but he pointed right back at her then swept his arm through the crook of her elbow. "In. I don't air my laundry on the front steps. Kate's front steps."

"No touching."

"Excuse me?"

"If I come in, no hugs, no fond embraces. No kissing."

"Furthest thing from my mind." He raised his hands in supplication and she stepped over the threshold and crossed the hall until she faced him from the far wall. "Let's sit down," he said.

"Last time you didn't want me near that living room."

"A picture's worth a thousand words."

"Nick—" Somehow he'd slung his arm around her.

"Relax, I'm just steering you in the right direction." As he urged her into the living room, she tried not to think about how warm he was and how just beneath the denim the fabric was a green plaid cotton. She glanced at the photos of Kate she'd seen on her first visit, but he pointed to the end table at the far side of the couch. There were more photos, these with a dark-haired, attractive man. In one he was holding Kip. Another was a family shot of the three of them. "That's Paul. Sunday I told you that Kip is named Nicholas for me and my dad. Truth, Shannon, but I'm not Kip's father, I'm his uncle. Kip is my nephew. That's Paul Goulding smiling at you from the eight-by-ten. Kip's father."

She was silent for a moment while she looked from photo to uncle. "That's it?"

"That's what?"

"If Paul is Kate's wife and Kip's father, then you're not grieving for your ex-wife?"

"Nope. Never been married."

"You're not...*raw*...from the divorce from Kate."

"No."

"Then you lied this morning."

"Yes, but that was out of self-preservation. See how wrong you were? You thought the lies were about being married, not being unmarried. This morning it was you who assumed I was newly separated. It's been your assumptions all along that have gotten me into this."

Fury whipped through her. She scowled and shoved. He teetered back on his bare feet and fell into the couch. "Whatever misconceptions I got were because you laid them at my feet you lying, cheating, miserable cretin."

"Wait a minute. I haven't been cheating on anybody. There's no wife, no ex-wife, no lovers, Shannon. One of the things I love about you is your candor. You're frank, fresh, gorgeous. You can protest all you want but that flush of yours has a vocabulary all its own. Gives me answers when you're nothing but a pack of questions. There you were this morning all flushed with concern over my misery. I thought if I embellished your misconception, it would keep you at bay. Shannon, I haven't been doing anything but trying to get you out of my system so I can concentrate on my job."

"Of all the egotistical platitudes. You make it

sound like I've been chasing you down Thurston Court.''

"You're here again, darling.''

"Don't you *darling* me.'' The damned flush started again, right up from her breasts and along her jaw. "Coming down here tonight does not constitute chasing. Somebody had to straighten out this mess. Admit it, you led me to believe you were newly separated, still smarting from losing Kate, still in pain.''

"Guilty.''

"You heartless snake. Why? If you're not married and you're not Paul, then why all this?'' She waved at the air. "Deception?''

"I told you. You're ruining my concentration.''

"Baloney.'' She yelped as he grabbed her wrist and tugged her down beside him.

"Look at me, Shannon.''

"Not for one second. It's far too dangerous.'' She did anyway. His expression was wide-eyed, contrite and as appealing as ever. "Talk, Nicholas Goulding. Start at the beginning and don't even inhale until you've reached the part where I'm standing at your door two minutes ago.''

"The beginning was Sunday and a trip to the zoo. My nephew Kip got lost then found by a green-eyed beauty with a garden full of geraniums and a heart of gold. You, Shannon, jumped to as many conclusions as I did. I thought you were married, you thought Kip was mine.''

"Why didn't you correct me?''

"You didn't say it in so many words. It didn't

come up at first. I guess I never explained because I didn't realize your mistake until everything began to snowball.''

She waited but Nick sighed and leaned back into the overstuffed upholstery. ''Continue,'' she muttered.

''What did it matter on Sunday? I didn't think I'd ever see you again. To me, you had a husband then. I'm working all day...''

''I thought you had Kip all day.''

''Working at baby-sitting. Who knew you'd be everywhere I turned, jumping to your own conclusions? Surely you don't expect a guy to explain or confess or straighten things out when you follow him up the stairs and right into his arms. Last night I knew damn well any confession would ruin the moment.''

''There wasn't any moment. Your remarks about my wanting to jump into bed with you were completely off-base.'' He was making her breathless.

''A guy can hope.''

''I referred to it as your ex-wife's bed. I remember that very clearly. You could have corrected me then, Nick.''

''By then you were burning me at the stake. No way was I going to give you any more fuel for that fire. Give me some credit. As an apology this morning I dragged the poor little guy to the shop for the puppet practice or whatever you concocted to get me to dinner.''

''Just one minute.''

He tapped his bare foot. ''I confess. I've used Kip

as Cupid. You weren't above doing it, either, toots. Admit it.''

''I've never used Kip.''

''An invitation for puppet testing got me to dinner.''

''Don't you dare suggest I made all that up. This morning in the workroom you saw what I wanted Kip for.''

''Let's dissect this morning in the workroom.'' He traced her burning cheeks with one finger.

''No touching. Remember?''

''Barely.''

She cleared her throat. ''Nick, I've heard Kip call you that daddy nickname. What did you do, conduct little training sessions? Bribe him? Tell him Paul was gone?''

''Never that. We made a little game.''

She shoved his hand away and jammed her fingers into her hair as she stood and looked down at him. ''Called 'When You See Shannon, I'm Daddy'?''

''I would have told you. Under cool, calm conditions I would have explained. We haven't had any. This morning when you decided it wasn't work that was keeping me from you, it was Kate, your mistake suited me fine. I let you think I was a grieving, wronged ex-husband so you'd leave me alone. There. I confess. That, darling Shannon, is the truth.''

''I never should have come back here tonight.''

''We've only reached this morning. You didn't want me to stop until I reached this moment.''

''I've heard more than enough.''

"Suit yourself." Nick Goulding was impossible to second-guess and this time he walked her back to the foyer. As she reached the dining-room archway, she glanced at the computer.

"Show me what's got you so busy."

"I don't think so." The edge in his voice was new, unlike any of the repartee.

"I really am interrupting aren't I?"

"You'll never know how much," he muttered. "No hugs, no fond embraces. No kissing." She looked at him for an explanation. He shrugged. "Quoting you, Green Eyes."

"Go back to your laptop and whatever work is in it."

"Damn good idea."

Her stomach knotted. As she walked back to the curb, Kip's baby-sitter Rachel suddenly called hello as she closed a car door. Shannon waved and hurried toward home. Finally around the bend and back at Three Thurston Court she threw her arms wide in frustration. She arched her back and stared at the stars. Desire still raced through her. Nick Goulding was high risk but there was no wife, no other relationship, Kip wasn't even his responsibility. She couldn't remember when she'd felt more alive, more in tune with her own feelings, good and bad. Her laugh was sardonic.

6

Until he reached Shannon's potted geraniums, Nick had no plan as he raced barefoot around the curve in Winchester Place and onto Thurston Court. She was on her front walk, barely illuminated by the glow of her curb lamp. The globe beside her front door was still dark. She was arching that glorious back and throwing her arms wide. She put her face to the stars and he thanked a few himself.

For one exquisitely arousing moment he watched her, unwilling to fight his body's response. The ache had built back in his sister's living room. Even ten feet away the woman continued to melt his bones. He managed a husky whisper as he called her name and tried not to startle her.

She turned, arms still wide. "Nick?" He reached her in four steps. She looked at his feet. "No shoes."

"No time."

"This is irresponsible. You mustn't ever leave Kip alone, not even sleeping. Not even for a moment."

"I ran into Rachel when I came out after you. She's sitting."

"You came after me? You nearly threw me out of

the house.'' She climbed the steps and put her hand on her doorknob.

''Not so fast. I'm here for one reason. You forgot one minor point in your stroll down Winchester Place tonight. When you arrived all fire and brimstone and righteous indignation, you said you learned about the Gouldings on the way down to see me. You must have been headed in my direction for another reason.''

''Long forgotten.''

''I doubt it.'' He listened to the crickets while she hedged.

''Forget it, Nick.''

''Not on your life.'' Even in the shadows he was hoping for another McEvoy blush. Under her brother's oversize shirt she seemed to be panting softly. ''All right, maybe you should know. I was unpacking and I found an old Jake O'Donnell column, something about telling a man outright what you want, no coyness.''

''Jake O'Donnell? Damn good advice, especially since this morning you gave me an earful of exactly what you don't want. Me within shouting distance, right?''

''Yes.''

''But of course you told me that right after kissing me like you wanted to melt my bones.''

''Never mind about melting your bones.''

''Mixed signals, puppet maker. Men have been writing columns about that for centuries. I'm just here after the truth, just as you were a while ago.''

She scowled. "To be honest, the O'Donnell column sounded like you, like advice you might agree with."

"The man gives great counsel."

"Don't be ridiculous. It was stuffing in one of my boxes. The man presumes he's an expert on women and he doesn't know the first thing about them. About us. He's infuriating more than he's even close to a decent sentiment."

"My mistake," he muttered.

"I admit this time I reread the column and I thought after treating you so badly at the shop..." She straightened her shoulders. "If you must know, when you said you were still raw, I was horrified at my cavalier behavior. You gave me the impression that you were still grieving, terribly hurt over the divorce. I came down tonight to apologize for being so insensitive, for hurting your feelings. I came to admit that, yes, I had used Kip as a ploy to get you to dinner."

"Why, Shannon McEvoy, you scheming female."

"Don't you dare talk to me about scheming. On the way I ran into a neighbor and when I stuttered over Goulding she said yes, Kate's last name is Goulding. You know the rest."

"I know damn little."

"Well you certainly know more than I do."

He shrugged. "You seemed so fond of Kip and jumped to so many conclusions. I honestly would have told you, meant to, in fact, before all the kissing upstairs. Shannon, more than once we've been headed in a very pleasant direction. No man with a normal testosterone level would have set the record straight and risked losing a chance with you.''

''I think it's time to cut through that baloney.''

''No baloney. Tonight you caught me in my boxers because I was going to bed early.'' He stopped and watched her shadowed figure. He stared and let his glance linger on the loose hair and tilt of her chin. ''Needing to get my work done, guilt and wanting to make things right between us kept me up all last night. Truth.'' He crossed his heart. ''Then there's this unrelenting ache.''

''Such a way with words.'' Her smile was so sudden it raised gooseflesh along his arms. ''You do give off a certain amount of heat.''

He laughed softly. ''Reciprocated on more than one occasion. That's the trouble. I meant every word at Kate's just now, but woman, you've been known to send out some powerful signals of your own. It's obvious that you've left me remembering every moment since you came to Kip's rescue. I am raw but it's not from any divorce. It's not from a torn heart or another woman. Please, Shannon,'' he said huskily from the back of his throat. ''Jake O'Donnell was right on the mark. Tell a man what you want.''

The shadows had pulled the color from her fair skin and wide eyes but there was no mistaking the sweet, dream-dipped expression on her face. He sank his hands into her hair and inhaled the faint familiar smell of her shampoo as he kissed her. Nothing in recent memory had tormented him this way.

The tiniest of moans, barely above the crickets and peepers and distant city traffic, escaped through her parted lips. She leaned back against her door, then slowly, as if she were fighting her own reluctance, she nestled and suddenly all those fabulous curves fit against the length of him. As he felt her arms slide around his back, he thanked his editor, the *Register,* heaven and every twinkling star over their heads that she'd read that column.

He felt his skin heat to the touch of her hands as they widened over his ribs and under his T-shirt. *Tell a man what you want,* he'd written. He was underwater and she was leading him to air. She kissed him back and melted his resolve along with everything else. Tomorrow he'd face the consequences. Charlie Hutchinson, *Three Rivers Magazine* and half-baked theories on single women could wait. He couldn't.

He kissed her again. This was no buss on closed lips. This was the top of Kate's stairs Tuesday night, the Time Out storage room this morning. It was everything he'd fantasized about since his first glimpse of her. He opened his hand along her jaw and found the steady beat of her pulse as he slid his fingers inside the worn collar of her oversize polo shirt. ''Room for me in there, too,'' he murmured as he skimmed her collarbone then moved one hand under the gaping shirttail.

''Evan's. Old…'' Her answer came in little gasps. ''You better get yourself home before all my new neighbors wind up pressed against their windows.''

''Or we could forget everything I said in the past

hour. The real solution is right inside. Think like a man, isn't that what Jake says? Take me up your stairs, Shannon. Let's finish what we've started so many times." She opened her door and his too-tight skin sizzled.

"Nick, Jake O'Donnell seems to think you men want honesty," she whispered with her hands pressed against his chest. "If he knew half a fig about women, he'd say that's all they want. Ever. You've been running from it since the moment I met you."

"Not tonight."

"Okay, tonight we got started. You made progress but the clock's ticking. The sitter's waiting. You have work to do. After the tongue-lashing at your sister's, I'm not going to be responsible for distracting you any further."

"I want you to," he managed to say, and her soft laugh settled over his spine. Her skin was hot where his thumb played over her ribs, or maybe it was his skin that burned as his knuckles grazed the lace cup supporting her breast. "I want you to so I can stop fantasizing and get you out of my system."

She pressed her fingers against his mouth. "Go back to your research and your computer. Believe me, twenty minutes under my sheets won't get me out of your system. Nick Goulding, I'm better than any fantasy."

The next morning under threatening skies, Nick dragged his tortured, exhausted self behind a trotting Kip as they reached the playground. Twenty minutes under Shannon McEvoy's sheets might have earned him a peaceful night. Instead he'd walked back to Winchester Place and stayed up half of it working out his rough draft, a damned good one. When he'd finally fallen into bed, it was to toss and turn in the same erotic Shannon dreams that had tormented him all week.

"Up, Tendaddy."

He lifted Kip onto the second rung of the kiddie bars and tried to concentrate. He was walking a tightrope narrower than any playground equipment. *Nicholas Goulding, sociologist.* Shannon now thought Paul Goulding was his brother when in painful fact Kate Hansen Goulding was his sister. As far as he could remember, that was the last of the deceitful little threads in the web he'd spun around himself, threads he could have explained away if only there weren't every chance in the world that truth about *Hansen* might lead her to the truth about his assignment, which inevitably would lead her to the truth about Jake O'Donnell.

Even his alter ego was spewing advice that had come back to haunt him. Back when he'd typed out, *Tell a man what you want,* he hadn't meant soul-stripping honesty. In the overcast haze of day the minor, inconsequential fact about his name pressed on him like a lead vest. He'd crossed the line, jumped the wall, snipped the barbed wire he'd strung between himself and the flushed, flirting, copper-haired package he was close to unwrapping. He was the one still tied up in knots.

He needed to tell Shannon who he was without inciting the wrath of Zeus, Venus, Athena and all other mythic personalties with a convoluted romance in their past. Of course he would explain. He'd envisioned it half the haunted night. He'd tell her in bed, while she lay in his arms—as soon as he figured a way that wouldn't catapult him back to Kip before he could zip his jeans.

With Kip safe in the sandy play pit Nick pulled his pad from his backpack. They were on a community playground in the North Hills, one he'd passed on the way to the mall. He was exhausted, bleary-eyed, but determined. Despite all his travels, nothing compared journalistically with the nuggets he'd gotten with Shannon. Although concentration on anything more than Kip was almost beyond him, there was always a chance that something brilliant would come to him in the way of a new angle for the article if he sat and took advantage of the opportunity.

He sat on the bench at the edge of Kip's turf and glanced at his notebook. "Tendaddy!" Nick waved and scribbled lists. Lists of his lies, fibs, fabrications just to keep his life straight. He took his eyes from Kip long enough to stare morosely at the Nicholas Hansen he'd printed but no brainstorm came to him. What came to him was a brunette with a golden retriever puppy.

"Mind if I share the bench?"

Not a bad opening for the article he thought as he shook his head and slid aside. "Not at all," he replied as Kip yelled for him to watch as he worked his way over a set of tires. "Great job," Nick responded as he glanced back at his notepad.

She dropped a quilted bag at their feet and ruffled the puppy's fur. "Mom's morning out?"

"Excuse me?"

She smiled. "We don't see many dads here, especially at this hour."

Jump at this, he told himself. He had the opening and there were half a dozen other moms or nannies or whoever they were settling in for what appeared to be their morning routine. He waited for his adrenaline to kick in, or his interest or his intellectual curiosity. Nothing. Hansen, he thought, you're a disgrace to Jake O'Donnell, a disgrace to manhood, a disgrace to the fine-tuned journalistic tradition of smoky rooms and two-fisted liquor and old Spencer Tracy movies. Hell, he was a disgrace to his former self. He stared at space.

"Barbie Catello," she was saying.

"Like the doll?" he replied with his eyes on Kip. Maybe there was grist for an article on women named for statuesque toys. He ran his hands through his hair and berated himself for waiting so long to meet the magazine deadline. His only hope with Shannon was to keep their relationship completely separate from his article, from any of his work, for that matter. That meant there was no hope. Shannon McEvoy and the spell she'd cast on his good intentions was the theme for the entire piece, and rough as it was so far, it was good, one of the best he'd ever written. No chauvinistic angle, no thinly disguised euphemisms. It was from his heart, what was left of it.

He sat there with Barbie's chatter and let reality sink in. He stared morosely at Kip. Tonight he should try to come up with something else, another angle, something unrelated to his personal agony just in case he could sell it to Charlie Hutchinson at the eleventh hour. A month ago he could have talked Hutchinson and his yuppie band of assistant editors into something more trendy: "Coffee Bars"; "Workout Centers"; "How to Find Single Women at the Automotive Center." Right about now he'd bet his box seats at the Civic Arena that his editor would only take what had already been promised. The issue was nearly in production.

He wondered if confession might work with Shannon. He could lay himself at her feet. Wouldn't she have to admit the whole rotten idea turned out to be a hoot? Hapless bachelor borrows baby as test subject. Any woman would see the humor in it. Any woman with a sense of humor.

Nick was still working new themes over in his head as he gave Kip a quick hose down before dinner. It was amazing that Kate only bathed him once a day before bed. No matter how he tried to keep the toddler clean, after every foray Kip was dirt, sand and grime from hair to sneakers, too filthy for the house and certainly too germy for the high chair.

The toddler was his usual end of the day self, exhausted and hungry—and not above soaking everything within the confines of the tiled room. Nick's concentration on his own problems dissolved as Kip got soap in his eye.

"Tendaddy to the rescue," he tried as he flushed Kip's startled face with a washcloth of clean water. "A good, healthy rescue is what we both need right about now."

"Hungry," Kip repeated as the two of them finally made it to the kitchen.

"You and me both." He pulled a graham cracker from its waxed paper wrapping and turned his back just long enough to spoon canned spaghetti into the bowl for the microwave. It was just long enough for Kip to reduce the rest of the pack to crumbs by stuffing half of them into his mouth and falling on the remainder.

"Dinner. I promise. Up you go." Into the high chair and out of harm's way, he thought as he stepped forward and flattened the package that had somehow made it beneath his boot.

The microwave beeped. He swore, stirred, tested and served. When Kip finally had dinner in front of him, Nick sat at the table next to him and skimmed his notebook. Barbie had been followed by Ashley and then Jennifer. There'd been two Emilys and a Kristen. No more animals or cartoon characters. No more enthusiasm or energy. He was sapped. Drained, frazzled, distracted.

Kip dropped his spoon from the high chair tray and used the tomato sauce on his plate for finger paint.

He got as far as designs on the toaster when Nick finally snapped to attention.

"Kip!" The toddler jumped at the sudden noise, knocking over his milk as his wail split the air. As Kip sobbed the white liquid puddled on the tray and dripped over the edge onto the floor. "Hasn't anyone told you not to cry over spilt milk?" he said as he sopped and wiped and cursed the situation he'd put himself in.

"Mommy."

"I know. We're both tired. Let's get you out of this seat."

"I want Mommy."

Despite frantic objections, Nick managed to get the exhausted bundle of spaghetti-covered energy into his arms, staining his shirt, hands and chin in the process.

The portable phone he'd taken to carrying in his hip pocket rang as he carried Kip up the stairs. It was Kate and he braced himself for her usual anxiety and concern. Day four and she was no better than day one. Neither was he. Kip fussed in his arms. "I'll call you back. Kip's covered in milk and spaghetti. We're on our way to the bath, second one in less than a hour. I don't dare put him down."

"He's still awake?"

Nick sighed. "Yes, Kate. I'm the one on my last legs."

"Nick, you need to be alert—"

"I know what I need," he snapped.

His sister's laugh surprised him. "Let me guess...a

good night's sleep, some time to yourself or a good woman to share the burden."

"Did I say Kip was a burden?"

"You haven't mentioned your grand experiment. Lots of grist for the article yet? Are women flocking to you, bachelor father?"

"Yes and yes. They're positively flocking."

"You've lost the lilt in your voice. You're either getting a real taste of parenthood and it's overwhelming you or the women out there are playing havoc with your plans."

"Go back to your idyllic vacation," Nick muttered. "If you must know I've got all the information and observation I need. Wrote a damn good rough draft, too, based on some episodes you, as a woman, would find hilarious."

"Your ineptness?"

"Let's just say I went into this expecting parenthood to be as civilized as a croquet match. What I've been getting is rugby, in overtime."

"Kip's an angel."

"Kip's a two-year-old. I've been rescued from my own ineptness. Never occurred to me that this experiment might take that turn, but darn if it isn't a better piece with me as the hapless bachelor."

"Disaster strikes Mr. Mom."

"Sort of. Witty, as I said, but it lacks something, maybe the usual Hansen sarcasm. As soon as I get Kip tucked in, I'm starting over."

"With the deadline breathing down your neck?"

"I need a fresh approach."

There was a pause and another soft chuckle that only his sister could get away with. "Missing something, Nick, or is one of your subjects apt to recognize herself and come after you with a meat cleaver?"

"Forget the women's intuition stuff."

"Don't say I didn't warn you."

"I'm hanging up, Kate. Your son's getting tomato sauce on the wallpaper."

Fifteen minutes later while Kip played with his bath toys, Nick leaned against the tub. His real torment lay in the disk downstairs in his laptop computer. The heart of his article, full of his signature wit and sardonic humor, hinged on Shannon McEvoy. He'd sat at his keyboard and shaped every episode and incidental conversation with her into gold. The rough draft was good, damn good. The genius lay in the turnabout. It rode on humor and the frailty of his bachelor behavior, the strength of hers. He'd used his writer's prerogative and exaggerated the episodes until Shannon was the perfect counterpoint. She'd kill him when she read it.

He'd disguised her physically but there was no reworking the facts. It was the truth that made the piece and when the piece made the newsstands she'd make papier-mâché out of him. He handed Kip a duck from the basket in the corner. He had two choices: lay his entire sorry life at Shannon McEvoy's feet and beg forgiveness or write another piece. Either way he needed two things he didn't have: time and his normal working routine. Something had to give.

Kip suddenly wailed again for Mommy and scrubbed his eyes. "I think it's time that we both visited your mommy, Kipster. It's time we got you back where you belong. You sure aren't doing me any good where you are." He kissed the top of his nephew's head. "And I can't see that I'm doing you much good, either."

By Friday morning Shannon had reminded herself a dozen times that she hadn't expected to hear from Nick. Hadn't they made a pact of sorts? Hadn't she been as emphatic as he? The man was gorgeous. The man was up to his tonsils in child care and under some sort of professional deadline. Of course he needed to be left alone. And who—or what—did she think she was by insinuating that she was better in bed than his fantasies? Her expertise in beds stopped at hospital corners on the top sheet and blanket. She should be relieved that at this rate he'd never come close to discovering what a fallacy her innuendos would turn out to be.

It wasn't the only behavior that embarrassed her. With the exception of his visit to the shop Wednesday morning, dinner on her patio, the grocery store incident and their volatile episodes at Kate's had all been initiated by her. By Saturday afternoon it was just this side of humiliating that the enigmatic sociologist had kept his word and kept his distance.

There was no nonchalantly walking past the Goulding condo in the hopes of another coincidence, either. Kate and Paul's cul-de-sac town house wasn't on the way to anywhere else. Instead, in the hopes that Nick and Kip might drive by on their way out of the complex, she'd taken to leisurely front garden perusal before work, late afternoon after work, before dinner, then after the dishes, coffee-in-hand. She'd done everything but pitch a tent and crawl into a sleeping bag. She was puttering now and if she gave her geraniums and perennials any more attention they would wilt from sheer pampering. Her backyard garden was neglected. Inside boxes still lay unpacked. Despite the routine, she hadn't laid eyes on either Goulding since Wednesday night.

Okay, the sociologist needed space. She just wished he'd said how much space and how long he needed it. She sighed and pinched a spent leaf from the cascading vinca, then went inside and called her brother to accept his invitation to Lake Scituate for the weekend.

She didn't return until Monday evening. Her flower beds had done fine without her. Molly Fraser, one of her suppliers of handcrafted dollhouse items, lived just west of the lake, which had given her the excuse to stay over last night and tie in the trip with a business call this morning. She looked forward to her occasional lunches with Molly and the purchase of Fraser Originals for the shop. Today even the idyllic country visit has been soured by her mood.

"A bit distracted this morning," Molly had teased. "Man troubles?"

Was she that transparent? She'd apologized, denied and grumbled all the more because Evan and Jeannie had accused her of the same thing Saturday night after exchanging glances when she snapped at her half brother's teasing about "Geranium Man."

She'd come home to an empty house still in disarray, a day-old Sunday paper and a single phone message from Karen Holland who wanted to stop by Time Out the next evening after work to discuss the profile she'd written. Shannon's self-proclaimed antidote to the disappointment was to call in a takeout order from the Jade Dragon. The restaurant was just up the block from the shop. Dinner would be waiting by the time she put away the box of exquisite miniature needlepoint pillows and rugs she'd bought from Molly. She didn't need Nick Goulding, she needed a proper meal. Sweet-and-sour shrimp with fried rice and broccoli would soothe what ailed her. Besides, there was always a chance she'd get a decent fortune out of the cookie.

The June weather was working its way up the thermometer toward a long, hot summer, she thought irritably as she hurried down Walnut Street. The aroma wafted onto the sidewalk as Shannon opened the restaurant door. She was ravenous and her stomach grumbled as she stepped around the handful of patrons waiting to be seated. Nick Goulding, wallet in hand, was standing at the cash register.

7

—————➤◄—————

"Shannon." He smiled as if they ran into each other daily while picking up Chinese food. "Something else we have in common."

"Hello, Nick." What else might be on his list eluded her. She watched him, all casual gorgeousness in those worn khakis and one of his polo shirts. He joked with the woman at the cash register. Profoundly witty no doubt, she thought as she watched him pocket his change. "Getting your work done?" she added.

"Yes, as a matter of fact. Worse than college. I've pulled a couple of all-nighters to make the deadline. Not much left of my brain power. The Jade Dragon is always my solution when I'm too tired to cook." He raised his bag in salute and jostled past the waiting diners as she turned from him and gave her name to the waiter. When she'd paid for her order and turned back around he was gone.

She left the restaurant grumbling. Nick had taken Kip to the zoo a week ago yesterday. It had only been a week but surely they were more than neighbors with the same taste in food. Her internal mumbling evaporated as the door closed behind her. Nick was leaning against a parking meter chewing on an egg roll.

"Couldn't wait," he called. His glance, the one that melted her insides, started to work its havoc.

"I've been away and didn't feel like cooking, either," she replied, wanting him to respond that he knew, that he'd stopped by over the weekend. Instead he took another bite of his egg roll.

"We're missing somebody," she mentioned.

"Kip? He's back with Kate and Paul. I drove down to High Pines Thursday and delivered him, safe and sound—and as clean as I could get him."

She frowned. "I thought you were baby-sitting for the week while they were on vacation."

Nick's expression changed. "I did say that, didn't I. I was. That is until they missed him too much. You know how new parents are."

"How's your project?"

"Thanks to my ungodly hours, finished."

She waited for some explanation. "I thought you wouldn't be able to start the research until you were finished with Kip."

"I've been juggling both. That's what's given me such a hard time. With Kip returned early, I had a chance to move back to my own place and get down to business."

"Washington's Landing, on the river?"

"I told you?"

"One of the few snippets of information you've let slip, Mystery Man." She expected another snappy retort, but he glanced down the cross street and finished his egg roll.

"My car's around the corner. Need a lift?"

"It's out of your way if you were heading home to the island."

He shrugged. "Come on. Let me drive you home before your dinner gets cold."

They drove the few blocks in what she interpreted as an easy silence. It was hard to tell with Nick muttering at the traffic and getting caught behind a city bus. She was determined to sit in silence and not do the obvious—invite him in to dinner.

As he pulled into Thurston Court and up to her curb, he finally turned to look at her, or more accurately, at the bag in her lap. "Any chance my fried rice and General Tso's chicken would complement whatever you've got in that bag?"

Ah, the hint she'd been waiting for. "It might. Is this where you're supposed to ask me over to the island to share it?"

"My place." He hedged visibly. "Dinner'll be cold by then."

She didn't reply that he'd been headed in that direction when she'd run into him. Instead she looked at her town house. "This where I'm supposed to invite you in to my place?"

"Yup. That was your cue."

"For dinner." She kept the questioning tone out of her voice.

"That, too."

She was supposed to smile or lower her eyelids or

add another clever response but she was out of cleverness and back into damp palms. Instead of a witty retort, she opened her door and slid out, babbling about dinner on the patio and putting on a pot of tea. Her need for clever repartee and forced chitchat was worse than the night he'd shown up without Kip. Pittsburgh was humid, but the air was heavy with far more than accumulating moisture. Innuendo and expectation hovered, crackled between them as she pulled plates from the cabinet and put water on to boil.

Nick accepted a glass of wine from an opened bottle she pulled from the refrigerator. ''Not bad,'' he said as he sipped.

''Do you study wines? Any favorites?''

He shrugged. ''I know what I like. I'm no connoisseur. One Christmas a while back Kate and Paul gave me a wine rack for Christmas and an elaborate book after I wrote a piece on—'' he seemed to stumble ''—New York's vineyards.''

''You're published?''

''Yes.''

''In anything I might come across?''

Nick sipped the wine, then sipped again. ''Depends on what you read,'' he said finally as he turned to the brown bags with the familiar logo. ''General Tso's chicken is in here somewhere and I got a vegetable dish of some sort.'' He opened the bags and busied himself lining up the white boxes on the counter.

The water had reached simmer and so had she. Without waiting for a full boil, Shannon put her favorite mixture of loose leaves into her ceramic pot and added the water to steep the tea. "Living on Washington's Landing must be handy if you row. I use the walking trails over there once in a while. Lovely spots for picnicking." She was rambling, but it kept her busy. Her arm grazed his sleeve as she reached for the teacups and set them on their saucers.

"Very," he said.

"Very?"

"Handy. Great view, too." He followed her as she took silverware and napkins out to the patio table. She knelt at the herb garden laid out along the brick of the patio by the former owner and pinched back some mint. "Takes over if you let it," she told him.

Nick was looking down at her in that searching way she knew all too well. "Shannon, do you want to talk about mint?"

She let a sigh escape and stood up. "Mint, sociology, Chinese cooking—this is where we talk, Nick, to soothe my nerves."

"Talk won't do much for mine." He put those hands into her hair, tilted her head back and kissed her, kissed her until desire was neck and neck with doubt. His expression was wide-open. Doubt ebbed. She loved this. She probably loved him. Did he know? Could he tell? Maybe he'd stand there and kiss her until she confessed. She smiled. Maybe she'd stand here and kiss him until he did.

"What?" he asked. "What's that Cheshire cat expression for?"

"I want some answers." She cocked her head and

tried to formulate the questions. Later. For the first time since she'd laid eyes on him, she let the heat follow its own course. Course, it did. Raced, surged, galloped from fingers to toes. All parts in between took up the beat of her heart as she kissed him back. His mouth was as warm as his hands and he tasted faintly of her wine.

"We've started this so many times," he murmured.

"Conversation?"

"No, I didn't mean conversation."

"I didn't think so. This is going to ruin my appetite," she murmured.

"What is?"

"Anticipation. Trying to figure out if you're going to make a pass at me."

"That's what this is, Shannon."

"Yes," she sighed. "I recognized it."

He laughed.

"And next comes roving hands," she continued. "And pulsing parts and the possibility that we're going to—" She waved at the air. "Whatever."

His look was pure analysis. "Yes," he said with a nod. "We're going to *whatever*. We're going to rove and pulse." His laugh was deep and affectionate. He pulled her hand to his chest and laid it flat against his heart. "You can start here." She loved him.

"And this is where we let dinner get cold and I invite you upstairs?"

"Darn right it is." He bent, scooped her into his arms and carried her the few steps to the kitchen door. "God, I've missed you. These past few days without

Kip, even lost in my work, I've wanted to share a sunset or a joke or feel you like this.''

''Did you know I was gone?''

He shook his head. ''No. I was holed up in my office.''

''And now?''

''Now? Before we get to the main course, let's make this an appetizer we'll never forget.''

She slung one arm around his shoulders and reached for her doorknob with the other. ''I'm five-ten, Nick. Put me down or you'll throw your back out and be left remembering this moment for a lot more than an appetizer.'' He set her down but she avoided his eyes. ''Nick?'' she continued somewhere along his collarbone. ''I regret some of the things I said a few nights back, at Kate's, on the couch.''

''You were angry. You had every right to be.''

''Not those things. The things about being better than any of your fantasies.''

''I'll let you know.''

Her laugh was small. ''That's what I'm afraid of. I was teasing because I didn't think we'd get this far, not with all the lecturing you've been doing, wanting me at arm's length and all.'' She blew stray hair from her eyes again and cleared her throat. ''Nick, I'm not exactly an expert in this department.'' Because he'd been staring at her the entire time, she finally looked at him.

He played with her hair. ''There's no baby-sitter waiting tonight. No Kip to rush home to, Shannon. We'll slow things down.'' He brought her hands to the waistband of his jeans. "You've already had a healthy glance at me in nothing much but my boxers. Help me out of this pair and show me those freckles you mentioned last Wednesday morning in your storage room, the ones I wasn't going to see anytime soon. That's my fantasy, Shannon, it's been my dream all week."

She watched the transformation in his handsome features. Love was in those blue eyes, she was sure of it. "I trust you, Nicholas Goulding," she sighed. "You're an amazing man."

Dinner was the last of the wine, Chinese food reheated in the microwave oven and tea she iced since it had cooled to room temperature. They ate by candlelight in the dining room because by the time they got around to food, she was in nothing but Nick's polo shirt and he was dressed in boxer shorts, red, this time, a cotton stripe.

She tried to get him to talk, but he wanted answers first. She rambled about her family and the shop and the move to Walnut Street. She described the hard work of making her dream a reality. He kissed her as she explained the hospital workshops and toy donations to the women's shelters.

They finished dinner, skewered the pineapple and found the fortune cookies. He broke his open. *You will find happiness in the unexpected.* "True enough," he murmured.

Shannon snapped hers open and laid out the tiny

slip of paper. *Seize the moment.* She did and it lifted him right off his chair.

"Talk about the unexpected."

"You know what Jake O'Donnell says about telling a man what you want."

"Or showing him."

"Would you mind if we practiced a little more? I'd like to work on some of the finer points of what you showed me." Nick smiled at her and ran his hand right under the shirt. He played over her ribs, up along her bare breasts. She arched as pinpoints of heat brought her to the edge of her seat. "I meant back upstairs," she whispered as she leaned forward and kissed him.

She didn't bother with a light. The security lamps and streetlights outside filled her bedroom like a full moon, bathing Nick in a pale glow as they entered the room. She didn't talk. Not a word this time, no quick retorts or clever innuendos.

She concentrated on the sound of Nick's steady, rhythmic breathing as she stood in the pool of window light. He smiled as he lifted the shirt up. Her hair lifted and tumbled back on her shoulders as the collar slid over her head. His breath caught, deep in his throat. With nothing but inches of June air between them, she reached around to the safest spot she could think of and slid her fingers slowly between his shoulder blades.

"Work your magic," he groaned as he closed his eyes and raised his face to the window. He arched his shoulders, straight, then straighter still as she traveled down his spine.

Heat poured from her as he kept the space between them. "It's your magic, Nick," she whispered. "Your patience and humor. There's so much I want to know about you. So much you have to offer."

She watched his chest rise and fall in quick, sharp breaths. He pressed his fingers against her lips and she dug her hands into his hair. Suddenly every inch of Nick Goulding was pressed, nuzzled, molded into her own curves. He held her, barely breathing, with one hand against the back of her head and the other across her back. "Shannon, I don't deserve this," he said against her temple. She felt him shake his head in a moment she could have sworn had little to do with their rising passion. She pulled back enough to look at him but he kissed her again, deeply and cupped her hips. If she'd had the strength she would have made love to him standing up, but her knees were weak and she ached for the mattress.

The covers were bunched at the foot of the mattress and pillows were piled in disarray at the headboard from the first round of lovemaking. Nick grinned and she laughed softly as they fell together. They played and teased until he suddenly knelt and kissed her eyes closed. Up here before dinner he'd found every one of her freckles. He traced them again in the dark with his mouth and his hands and she touched, stroked, opened her hand on his ribs and felt his sharp intake of breath, then the thunder of his heart and the steady rise and fall of his chest. Nick's touch, touching Nick.

It was impossible to tell which aroused her more. Nothing else had ever felt this good.

She told him in laughing, gasping, incomplete sentences as she gave herself up to him. He paused. It was impossible to read his expression in the dark but for a fraction of a moment she felt his glance. He hesitated, as if perched on the edge of a cliff.

''Shannon.'' He said her name between gritted teeth. Whatever else he murmured was lost in the thunder of her own pulse and then they lost themselves completely. She loved Nick Goulding. She gave up her heart as he cradled her long after reality returned.

For long, blissful moments, Shannon lay still, smiling at the ceiling. Nick was quiet, his hand dead weight on her thigh. Sometime in the middle of the lovemaking the air conditioning had kicked on. In another minute she'd be downright cold. She lay there contemplating breaking the mood by reaching for the covers or getting up and into something appropriate. Clothes? Nightgown? The shower? It was barely nine-thirty. Were they in bed for the night? Surely he intended to stay. She had no idea what protocol demanded. She sat up, opting briefly for clothes and a clean kitchen.

Nick stirred and surprised her by sitting up as well. ''Feels like Saturday,'' he said sleepily. ''Wish it were.'' More surprise; he snapped on the bedside light. She turned, suddenly self-conscious and continued across the room to her closet, aware that his eyes never left her, hoping she gave the impression that walking nude in front of a lover was the most natural thing in the world.

"Love that blush," he said.

She pulled her silk knee-length robe from the hook and wrapped it around her, trying not to fuss self-consciously with either the tie or her hair. "There are some leftovers that should go into the refrigerator."

"I'll give you a hand before I go." So much for protocol. She must have looked crestfallen because Nick's expression softened. "Hate to." He stood up, buck naked and still gorgeous. "But I row at dawn, before work. I'd have to get out of here about five in the morning to get home for my stuff and over to the boathouse. I wouldn't want to wake you, either."

"You don't owe me an explanation."

He stared at her for a minute, eye to eye this time. "I owe you plenty, darling," he said softly. He worked himself back into his jeans—without a blush and without any further comment.

She went downstairs ahead of him. She let him putter for a moment, but the harsh light of the kitchen dredged up her self-consciousness. She wanted to be back under the covers and hold on to her satiated contentment. She wanted to talk, probe, discover a million more things to love about Nick. He was his usual pensive self as he insisted she keep the leftover chicken and rice. She showed him where to put the wine bottle for recycling. They could have been two strangers in a lunch line.

"You keep alluding to owing me and not deserving

this,'' she blurted before she lost her nerve. ''I don't know what you mean.''

Nick leaned against the counter and ran his hand through his hair. ''You're so trusting, Shannon.''

''I shouldn't trust you?''

''You should. Of course you should. I'm feeling guilty about using Kip to play cupid, about not explaining—things earlier.''

''Staying at your brother's house?''

''Using Kate's place, yes. That's part of it.''

''Using Kip?'' She smoothed her hands over his shoulders. ''Nick, no harm's been done. I'm sure Kip thinks he had a wonderful adventure last week with his Uncle Tendaddy. Surely if Kate and Paul didn't trust you they never would have left their only child in your care.''

He nodded but there didn't seem to be much relief in his expression. Pressing Nick to open up under these conditions wouldn't get her anywhere. ''Go on home,'' she said finally. ''Even I can see how tired you are.''

He pulled her into an embrace. ''Thanks. I'm completely exhausted.''

She raised an eyebrow. ''You'd better be.''

He laughed. ''You have no idea what a pleasant fatigue this is.''

''Oh, yes, I do,'' she replied and pushed him gently to the front door. Nick grew pensive again. She waited.

''I'll call you,'' he said finally.

"See that you do." She hoped he caught the lilt in her voice.

"How about tomorrow night? Dinner—or something?" His devilish grin was back.

"No more something. Dinner would be nice but I want conversation out of you. Can't be tomorrow, though. I have an appointment at five and my puppet program at Children's Hospital after that." She held back suggesting Wednesday in case she appeared too eager. Then again when you'd made love twice in one evening to the likes of Nick Goulding there didn't seem to be much left in the eager department.

"Wednesday?" Maybe he was the eager one.

"I think Wednesday's fine. What's your number on the island in case I need to get in touch with you?"

He told her and started down the front steps. She waved and closed the door before he reached his car. No sense in making him think she was so lovesick she had to watch until he was out of sight. She was, of course, and the last place she wanted to be was upstairs alone in her bed for the rest of the night.

A million graphic images flooded her as she finished in the kitchen, images sure to ruin her sleep and destroy her day tomorrow if she didn't make peace with herself and her behavior. She was too keyed up to sleep so she showered and washed her hair, styled it and finally pulled on an oversize T-shirt to sleep in. She changed the sheets, straightened the bed, sighed and smiled as she shook out the pillows. Nick Goulding needed work in the conversation department, but in every other aspect he was perfect, so perfect it made her blush.

Before she snapped off the light, she grabbed her address book and opened it to G. She drummed her fingers. Why hadn't she written his number down right away? She remembered the exchange being 555 but the rest escaped her...8277 or 7728 or something close. She grabbed the phone book. Five Gouldings were listed. Paul and Katherine H. had identical listings on Winchester Place, David in Point Breeze and two in the suburbs. None of them was Nicholas or even N. She frowned and tried Directory Assistance in the hopes that he'd moved in since the last phone book was printed. She hung up the phone even more baffled. There was no Nicholas Goulding or N. Goulding listed or unlisted in the greater Pittsburgh area.

It was raining when she awoke and down to a drizzle by the time she opened Time Out. Late morning brought a downpour forcing customers to arrive hunched and shaking umbrellas. Did Nick row when it rained? Had he slept in after all? Was he at his office? Home at a computer? She tried to disguise morning-after guilt with curiosity but it made her cheeks hot to think she'd been so blatantly intimate with someone who still raised more questions than answers.

Tomorrow evening couldn't arrive soon enough. Nick, no doubt, had a logical explanation about his phone, but damned if she could come up with what it might be as she puttered over inventory, waited on customers and laid out supplies for her evening class.

In typical Pittsburgh fashion, the sun broke out by late afternoon and by the time Karen Holland arrived at five, the sidewalk cafés were back in business and the steamy, puddled streets were bustling.

"My piece on you came out very well if I do say so," the journalist said as they ordered a light supper and sipped wine at the nearest bistro. She opened her leather-bound portfolio and pulled out a sheaf of papers. "Want a look at the copy of the mock-up?"

"Did you mean for me to proofread it for accuracy?"

Karen shook her head. "Actually, Shannon, I'm here for another reason. My editor, Charlie Hutchinson, was very taken with your story, and your photograph for that matter. He's proposing that I talk you into accepting the honor."

"What honor?"

Karen sipped. "Of being named one of this year's Most Eligible Women."

She must have looked as flabbergasted as she felt because Karen laughed. "Scout's honor. The committee doesn't pick until the very last minute to keep it quiet. This is the week. You'd be in great company. Of the five women, you'd be the youngest. The oldest is May Hemming, sixty-six. When she was widowed she took over her husband's sheet metal plant in the Hill District and set up a training program for school dropouts."

"I can't compete with that! I don't run around to

charity events. My name doesn't show up in the social columns. I'm only twenty-eight with a small business.''

''And a big heart. That's what the committee's after to balance the more obvious philanthropy. I admit it does put you and your work in the limelight, but not much more than the article you've already agreed to. It will generate more volunteers for the hospital and more customers for you.''

''I don't know,'' she said as their waiter set down supper.

''Eat,'' Karen replied. ''Think it over. There's one more thing. If you agree, you'll need to pose with the rest of the group for the magazine cover.'' Karen poked her fork in her salad and laughed. ''Don't look so pale. Why don't I change the subject?''

Shannon laughed. ''Maybe you'd better.'' She nibbled at dinner while Karen talked of other pieces she'd written, her trip to Africa to profile Pittsburgh's medical missionary and then falling in love with him. ''Now that would make a great article,'' Shannon replied trying to relax.

''Wouldn't it. Me, of all people. The original romantic cynic.'' She laughed. ''Are you a Jake O'Donnell fan?''

Shannon shrugged. ''What woman is? I swear he writes half his columns just to irritate female readers, if he has any.''

''He has plenty. Did you ever read his piece on women and their wedding rings?''

"As if we have any way to tell when a man's married when half don't wear rings at all."

Karen wagged her ringed fingers. "I inspired it. I met him at a conference. Fell head over heels like every other woman. He's a rower, so I trumped up an article on the boathouse he could help me with. Did it just to hang around him. Spent the most romantic evening, right down to a roaring fire. The works. I was due to leave for Malawi the next week and boy, did I wait for that phone to ring."

"Nothing?"

"Nothing. Of course little did I know what awaited me at that dusty clinic half a world away."

"Love does crop up in the most unexpected places. Women fall in love with the guy? From his photograph he doesn't seem like your type. Older—" She tried for something diplomatic.

Karen was pulling another tear sheet from her bag. "He's thirty-one, actually a year younger than I am. Speaking of Nick Hansen, he wrote a wonderful piece for this *Three Rivers Magazine* issue you're in. Hilarious."

"I thought you were talking about Jake O'Donnell."

"Nick Hansen is Jake. You didn't think I liked that old codger with the cigar in the photo?" She laughed. "You are new in town. Nick took over the column when Jake died. Believe me, Nick's a lot easier on the eyes than the real Jake, half his age, too. He kept Jake's byline and head shot to stay anonymous but it's the worst kept secret in Pittsburgh."

"You make it sound like he should be on the Most Eligible list himself."

"Don't think Charlie Hutchinson doesn't try his darnedest every year. Nick won't touch the honor. Might blow his cover. This year to keep Charlie happy he's written a great piece under his own name. It's all about using a two-year-old to meet women." She chuckled again. "That night I interviewed him at the boathouse and we talked about wedding bands, I mentioned that women are always suckers for guys with kids. You know, single dads, struggling to be Mr. Mom gets the maternal hormones raging. Sympathy, empathy—who knows. Anyway, that son of a gun borrowed his nephew and tried it out. 'Borrowed Baby,' he's called it. I gather everything went wrong because the little boy was such a handful. Ran off on his way to the zoo, lost his shoe in the grocery store… He goes on and on about one gal he kept running into. Smashed geraniums."

Shannon's chest was on fire. "What geraniums?"

"Being planted by a perky little blonde, barely up to his chin, he wrote. She wagged her finger, did a schoolmarm proud. Lectured him up one side and down the other. I think he compared her to a mother grizzly, claws drawn. He calls the baby Evan and documents the experiment in that Hansen style. He's a darn good writer. It was my idea, but I never would have given it the self-deprecating twist that makes it shine."

"Evan? Mother grizzly?" The flush had reached

her scalp. "Go back," she insisted. "Back to Nick Hansen and the boathouse. He rows?"

"A physique to die for. He rows and helped me research a piece on the sport. For a few days there, I'd been hoping for a little more than oars, shells and river launches, as I said."

"So Jake O'Donnell is really this Nick Hansen person."

"Yes. As a matter of fact, I ran into him last week right across the street. He hinted that he was in the midst of the project. Trying to keep it quiet till it hits the newsstands, I guess. Probably forgot that I was the inspiration." She laughed. "You have to watch out for us writers. We're known to take inspiration wherever we can find it. He had the little boy with him. Kip was his name. He changed it to Evan in the piece."

"Nick's name is Hansen" was all she could manage to say.

"Yes."

"Well, now that I know all the intrigue, I'll have to read his column with a different eye." Did she sound casual? Intrigued? Amused? Winchester Place. Goulding. Jake O'Donnell. "Sounds like the perky little blonde gave him hell," she muttered. No more than a complete stranger and she'd made love to him in her own bed, twice. She was desperate to pump Karen for more details on the sordid, duplicitous, fabricated life of Nicholas Whoever-he-was. Writers were thicker than thieves. Writers were thieves. She stuffed a forkful of salad into her mouth and hoped she digested it more smoothly than she was ingesting the information being laid out by Nicholas Hansen's fellow journalist.

Karen sipped her wine. "You'll love the piece when it comes out. Even those of us who growl over his Jake O'Donnell stuff have to admit that Nick's a crack writer. He's got a real way with words."

Didn't he just.

8

Wednesday at noon Nick slapped the *Pittsburgh Register* overstuffed manila envelope on his kitchen counter. Jake O'Donnell/Nick Hansen was scrawled across it in felt-tipped marker by the fledgling journalist who had the job of culling and sorting the mail addressed to the Living pages. He cursed the packet and grabbed a bottled iced tea as he headed for his deck.

Yesterday's rain had cleared the air, if not his head. Even a gut-busting two-thousand-meter piece on the ergometer at dawn hadn't done a thing to help. For two nights alone in his own bed he'd berated himself for not coming clean.

Next time, another day, when the time's right had been his litany for a week. Shannon McEvoy's doe-eyed, trusting confession that she might have exaggerated her expertise had laid the perfect opportunity at his feet. All those long, sensual, arousing moments when he'd held and reassured her would have been the perfect time to whisper his own confessions. In their short, incredible evening he'd trampled every opportunity. Hadn't she asked him about himself? Hadn't she initiated conversation?

Together in the dark he could have made light of his lies, flattered her, thanked her from the bottom of his scheming heart for her inspiration. He'd intended to explain but Shannon McEvoy made it impossible to think straight. She matched him in height, in wit, in determination. Just looking at her was better than a sunrise row on a fall morning. He was a master of vocabulary and words failed him. The minute he was within arm's length of her his body ran on pure adrenaline.

When had he told her he was raw? Last Wednesday? Damn right he was raw. He felt like a Laurel Highlands trout fillet, skinned, boned and slapped on a grill to fry. He winced while he watched his beloved river. He'd left her still entangled in his lies. No man could fault him. No guy in his position would have taken a chance at rejection after her green-eyed glances and witty innuendo.

A tugboat honked its air horn and he watched the coal barge inch its way past the island. He pressed his cold drink against his forehead. Shannon had been right on the money about something far more important than any sexual expertise. Making love to her had done nothing to get her out of his system. He kicked a pebble under his moccasin as he pulled the deck chair to the railing. It wasn't an early call on the river that had forced him back to the island Monday night. He'd even lied about that. It was astonishment. One incredibly erotic evening in her arms, in her bed, had whetted an appetite he could barely fathom. It aroused him now just remembering her in the candlelight, tousled and dreamy-eyed as she ate Chinese food in nothing but his shirt, reaching for him all over again. He pressed the bottle back to his temple.

The cool pragmatic Shannon would skewer him like shish kebab. Shannon under the sheets at her most vulnerable and their most intimate was his only hope. Tonight he'd confess; she'd listen with her heart. Tonight. Tonight. Tonight. He'd make her dinner, take her up to the loft for the view and bare his fraudulent soul as she ran her fabulous fingers over him.

Nick swore again; not his loft, no bed here. Every loose piece of mail, every diploma and award had Hansen on it. It had to be Thurston Court and her bed again while he bared his soul. He'd take her out to dinner, but he'd have to maneuver her back to her place until she understood everything, just until she forgave him.

His reverie was interrupted by the sound of the doorbell. It took two deep breaths to clear his head and then he went back through the kitchen and living room and opened his front door. Shannon stood in front of him in the shadow of the porch overhang. She had on the same midcalf jumper she'd worn the day he took Kip to the shop and the breeze played with it as it had the week before.

"Hello, Nick."

"Well, hi" was the best he could do. He looked

over his shoulder as if some piece of furniture might suddenly give away his identity. "What a surprise."

She nodded. "I'm full of them. Actually I'm terribly sorry to bother you in the middle of the day, but you mentioned that you sometimes work at home. I took the chance that I'd recognize your car or a neighbor could tell me which place was yours."

Guilt swept him again. Obviously the sight of his Jeep in the driveway had saved him. A neighbor would have told her there were no Gouldings in the complex. He pulled her into a hug and kissed her. As always, she smelled wonderfully of her shampoo or cologne or whatever it was that had stayed with him the rest of Monday night and now tortured his memory. "I'm looking forward to tonight."

"That's why I'm here. We need to talk."

"You should have called."

"I lost your phone number and crazy as it sounds, Directory Assistance swears you don't exist."

Oh what a tangled web we weave. "You must have gotten a trainee or something," he tried lamely.

"I guess I did."

She bought it? "Five-five-five, eight-seven-seven-two is my number." He sweated bullets while she fumbled with a pencil and scrap of paper in her purse.

"I have a conflict tonight and I didn't know how else to reach you, so here I am."

"If dinner's off, how about later, after you're finished—whatever it is that's a conflict. I'll meet you at your place."

"I don't think so. I was hoping we could exchange

dinner for lunch. A picnic," she was saying. "Since there are so many wonderful spots out here, I threw a few things in a basket just in case I found you."

Getting her away from the house was an excellent idea. He closed the door behind him. "Grab the basket. I know just the spot." She stepped back and cocked her head with a look that seemed to be half surprise. He grabbed her hand and led her down the steps before he had time to analyze the other half. She took a basket from the back seat of her car and he walked her along the jogging path with it between them. She asked about the boathouse. He pointed out the channel where he started his morning and the bridges all rowers used as course marks. "Someone said there are more bridges in Pittsburgh than Venice," he added.

"I believe it." Her usual wit was missing but the walk to the end of the island was pleasant. The breeze was strong and kept the hot air moving. He led her through a patch of woods and over to a secluded wedge of grass on the edge of the bluff that fell dramatically to the water.

"Shannon, Monday night was wonderful." There, somehow he'd make that a lead-in to more.

"I know." She opened the basket and laid the lid back. It was one of those sophisticated wicker ones lined in gingham with flatware, corkscrews and linen napkins. There wasn't a plastic utensil or paper bag in sight. His body stirred. This was no spur-of-the-moment island stop off. No wonder Shannon seemed lost in thought. She had an agenda. A smile burst from him as she laid down a checkered blanket, opened the butcher paper that wrapped deli sandwiches then sat two goblets on the grass. Wine would be good, loosen them both up, make her receptive to some confessions and lovemaking, both from the heart. He could at least explain about his name. A good place to start.

"No wine," Shannon said as she pulled out a thermos and filled their glasses with pale pink liquid. "Puts me right to sleep in the middle of the day and I have a meeting at the shop with my accountant. I did bring some pretty good tea. Herbal." She poured and handed him a glass. It tasted like weak, watery cough syrup with an undercurrent of lemon.

Shannon raised her glass. "Let's have a toast. To Evan and Kip and all the chaos that brought us together."

His diaphragm muscles contracted. "To Evan and Kip," he replied. *Speaking of your brother, I borrowed his name, he should be saying. I needed a pseudonym for Kip. I was using him for an article when we met, using him, using you. Of course I disguised you, too...* "Mesmerizing isn't it" was all he could manage to say as she kept her eyes on the river. A glass or two of some cheap Chablis would have helped.

"Mesmerizing," Shannon repeated. "Have you read Jake O'Donnell's latest column?"

"This week's?" *The one I wrote before I screwed up my entire existence?*

"You know I'm no fan of 'Since You Asked,' but

every once in a while he redeems himself—just enough to keep me reading his column. Must work for a lot of women. Savvy guy.''

"He needs his readership and his ratings. Staying in syndication's no easy task. From what I've been told,'' he added hastily.

"This week he goes on about expectations. A woman asked him to what he thought was a beer fest and jazz session on one of the riverboats. Turned out to be a string quartet and finger sandwiches.''

"Poor guy.'' He turned and tried to collect his thoughts as a train and its freight made its way along the riverside tracks.

"You can hardly blame him. Out on the river on a hot summer night is the perfect place for great jazz and maybe some samplings from the local breweries.''

He looked back at her. "You are full of surprises.'' The moment held. Shannon was looking at him with a solemn, placid expression that was as expectant as Monday night, if not as passionate.

"Expectations. That Jake O'Donnell,'' she was saying, which made him cringe. He glanced at his watch and moved closer. "You didn't come all the way over here with a packed hamper to talk about newspaper columns,'' he whispered as he nuzzled her ear. He let his mind wander as she ran her fingers around his jaw and played with his hair.

"How much time can you spare,'' she whispered back.

For you, Shannon, a lifetime. "As long as it takes."

"As long as what takes? To get me behind the rhododendron?"

"It was a slip of the tongue. But as long as you brought it up, there's a completely secluded spot around that bend." He nodded toward the sunlit patch of grass. Progress. A little more romance would soften the atmosphere and Shannon. He laughed and tried to kiss her.

She straightened up and moved his hand. "I've brought up a number of things without any response whatsoever. Now you expect me to jump into the bushes with you?"

"A guy can hope," he tried to joke.

"Yes, well, so can a woman, Nick."

He was thoroughly confused. "Shannon, I was kidding. I didn't really mean I wanted you, I expected you to, not over there in the bushes—"

"What do you really mean, Nick? When have you ever known what I wanted without my hitting you over the head? Honesty's what I want. Let's start with that before we get back to what we never should have gotten to in the first place." She knelt and began stuffing the picnic basic.

"Shannon, stop."

"It's a little late for that. Stop should have been Monday night."

"Look, you're here at my door with a picnic basket all packed. This wasn't some spontaneous moment.

You thought this scheme out. I'm just playing along for the ride...loving it.''

"Scheme?''

"Poor choice of words.''

"You're darn right.''

"Plan. Whatever you've planned.''

She stood up and yanked at the cloth until he rolled off it. A piece of sandwich bounced and disappeared over the bluff. "You're confusing the hell out of me.''

She glared. "Maybe it's about time. You've done nothing but confuse the hell out of me since we met.'' As he scrambled to his feet she pushed him back down. "Don't get up. Don't even think about walking me back to the car. Stay here and think about how you've kept me in the dark all week.''

She was glaring, burning holes in him while he waited and tried to figure out which omissions she was referring to. "About my last name being Hansen, not Goulding? There's a perfectly good explanation why I waited to tell you.''

Shannon brushed pine needles from her dress. "Excuse me, Nick, you haven't told me. What few facts and pitiful knowledge I have came from dragging it out of you. Do you need reminding? First you were a single father, then married, then grieving from a fresh divorce, then an uncle, all as a sociologist named Goulding. You lived on Winchester Place. Whoops, my mistake, Washington's Landing.'' She held up her fingers as she ticked off each accusation. "Worse, to discover the truth behind any of this, I've had to ask every question. I've watched you hedge. If it were up to you I'd still be in the dark.''

''I was getting around to the rest. I was hoping tonight things might mellow out. We'd have a nice dinner together and I could finish explaining.''

''Mellow out in my bedroom? Certainly not in yours. Back there at your place you couldn't get me away from your front door fast enough.''

''An hour ago I thought you thought my name was Goulding.''

''All right, I had a scheme. I've been sitting out here for half an hour feeding you gourmet sandwiches and hints broad enough to choke a horse. Jake O'Donnell, Jake O'Donnell, Jake O'Donnell. Why couldn't you at least have told me that much?''

It was impossible to reply. If she didn't know about the magazine article, now was not the time to explain that there was even more. ''I try to keep my private life separate from my professional.''

''Don't you dare try to convince me that the rest of the world knows you as Goulding. And while we're on that subject, how are you related to Paul and Kate or did you just make all that up, too?''

He put one hand out in supplication. ''Paul's not my brother. Kate is Katherine Hansen Goulding, my sister.''

''For the life of me I can't figure out why you had to lie about that one.''

''I didn't. It was your conclusion that I was related to Paul and it was just easier not to correct you.''

"Because then you would have had to explain about being *Hansen* not *Goulding*."

"Guilty as charged," he tried as she picked up her picnic basket.

"I'm leaving."

He stood up and shoved his hands into his pockets. "That's been my biggest fear. That's what's kept me from telling you."

"Cut the melodrama, Nick."

"Can you blame me?"

"Damn right I can blame you. I blame you for all of this."

"*This* is exactly what I was afraid of. You find out the truth, you're gone like a startled rabbit."

"So it's a rabbit now? I thought I was a grizzly with claws drawn."

Bull's-eye. She'd laid the last of her aces on the table. He was a dead man. He wanted to ask how she'd gotten from not being able to find his phone number to knowing he was Jake O'Donnell to "Borrowed Baby" but Shannon was steaming and he wasn't about to risk being tossed over the bluff and into the river just to satisfy his curiosity.

There was nothing but scorn in her expression as she gathered her things together. "I should have known from the start you weren't a sociologist. That would have implied that you had some knowledge of human behavior. I could have handled the truth, Nick. There are worse things in the world than being a prizewinning columnist, even a sexist, chauvinistic one. It's the deception I can't handle, the fact that

you've let every single lie drag out until I pounded
the facts out of you. You never offered me an ounce
of truth on your own.''

''Monday night I—'' He tried to get up.

She pushed him back to the grass. ''Don't even
think about moving till I'm off this island and don't
dare mention Monday night. I made love to a complete and total stranger.''

She left him. Packed up the picnic and stamped off
without so much as a glance over her shoulder. Nick's
mood went from apprehensive to black. Bad to worse
didn't begin to describe his situation. He was a master
at instinct. Intuition gave him themes for his column,
success on the water. Hell, he was no novice at main-
taining relationships by following what felt right. He
should have acted, confessed, come clean back when
he was muttering about it in the sandbox with Kip.

Where Shannon was concerned nothing felt right,
not what he'd done and not what he'd tried to undo.
She'd forced him to scramble like a sorry teenager.
Within hours of her departure he tried to get her at
work. He called Time Out; Meg said she was with a
class. That night he called her at home and got nothing but her answering machine.

Could a woman like Shannon McEvoy love a man
who groveled? Even laying apologies at her feet was
impossible if she refused any contact with him. He
had to come up with something more sincere and he
had no clue what that might be.

When the phone rang Friday it jangled his nerves

like an electric shock. "Hansen," he said, praying the reply would be some witty, forgiving retort about Goulding.

"So Nick, how about that dinner?" He recognized the laugh. "It's Karen Holland. Steve and I thought we'd grab something tonight with some jazz in the Strip district. I've just put the final touches on an article for the Most Eligible issue of *Three Rivers* and I'm coming up for air. Charlie gave me a look at your piece, by the way. You did use my idea. Of course the writing and self-deprecating humor is pure Hansen. Hilarious. When I ran into you on Walnut Street you said you'd explain. Grab a date and we could all celebrate."

He forced himself to accept. Anything to get his mind off his misery. "Tell me what you wrote," he added just to keep another human being on the line.

"Mine's a straight profile on Shannon McEvoy, one of our up-and-comers around town, a great looking redhead who owns her own toy shop on Walnut Street and parlays her talent into volunteer work with the little patients at Children's Hospital. Quite a gal. Old Charlie Hutchinson liked it so well he wants her on the list. Assigned me to get her. Took some doing over a working dinner Tuesday night, I can tell you. Worth it. Charlie thinks I'm a genius. Forget I mentioned her name, though. You know how our editor is about leaking the names of his precious Most Eligibles."

Nick's heart stopped well before Karen stopped talking. The pieces of the puzzle fell painfully into place. "I've forgotten her name already," he promised. Fat chance.

She laughed. "Good boy. You never heard it from me. Forget I mentioned it."

He agreed, chatted aimlessly and drummed his computer table the minute he hung up. Every bit of investigative instinct kicked in as he grabbed his desk calendar. Karen Holland had interviewed Shannon McEvoy earlier in the month. Monday night Shannon had made love to him as if there was no tomorrow. Karen and Shannon had dinner together Tuesday night. Wednesday the one-woman hurricane showed up at his door, canceled dinner, set him up with her trumped-up picnic, caught him at his own game and let him have it with both barrels. Now there was no tomorrow.

It was obvious that Karen had mentioned him, his article, something that kept the information flowing over her dinner with Shannon. It was also obvious that Shannon must not have shown any reaction, otherwise Karen would have called sooner or mentioned it just now. At that moment what he didn't know about the wiles of women would fill the Pittsburgh phone book. What little instinct he still trusted told him to keep quiet himself and he had. Instead of any gut-wrenching confession to his fellow journalist, Nick finished his conversation with her, hung up and dialed his editor at *Three Rivers Magazine*.

Tuesday Shannon waited self-consciously and concentrated on the spectacular early evening view from

Greta Mattson's photography studio at South Station. Soon the riverboats would fill for the dinner cruises along the Monongahela on their way around the Point. The cityscape gleamed from the other shore. She wondered if Nick had rowed that morning, not that she cared. Not a fig.

The stylist for the *Three Rivers Magazine* layout had called with instructions. For the group shot with the five other women, she was to dress in something indicative of her personality. For the magazine cover that was to include all dozen of them, six men and six women, she was to wear something appropriate for evening. The makeup artists had done spectacular things with her cheeks and eyes and voluminous things with her hair. No McEvoy would recognize her and she wasn't about to tell any of them until the issue hit the stands at the end of the summer.

She'd posed good-naturedly for the casual layout in slacks and a silky blouse that draped well and she hoped showed off her hair, by far her best feature. She'd finished posing as the men trickled in from the next room, as much a mix in age and ethnic background as the women. According to the assistant, the next shot would be the cover, all twelve of them, then she was free to leave as the men posed by themselves.

While the props assistant draped a white fabric over a short stepladder and changed the backdrop to a spectacular shot of Pittsburgh at night, she left to change into her evening outfit. She'd splurged on a slip of a black V-neck cocktail dress from the designer dress shop across the street from Time Out.

Never mind that she'd bought it the morning after the disastrous picnic. Never mind that she was sure that the one person guaranteed to see this issue was Nick Hansen. Let him eat his heart out. Hers was in pieces.

She came back with the women, some in long ball gowns and two in short dresses like hers. Her cocktail dress skimmed her knees. Demure, she thought, and out of character for the owner of a toy store. The men were in dinner jackets and the stylist had already begun to pose them. One had a hand in his pocket, pulling the jacket away from his pleated dress shirt, another had his arms crossed over his chest. The stylist was fussing with a third. She undid his bow tie and opened his collar as if she wanted to jump right in the shirt with him. Next she had him sling his tuxedo jacket over his shoulder with his thumb. She was working on Nick Hansen.

9

The shock of seeing Nick sent the flush right into Shannon's cheeks, scalp and, she realized as she forced herself not to cover it, down into her cleavage. Instead she gritted her teeth. She tried to convince herself that this was pure anger, except that anger didn't feel tingly and sweet and breathless all at the same time. The most casual gesture she could come up with was a toss of her hair. She felt rather than saw Nick turn and stare.

They were all introduced to each other by the assistants. She shook hands, smiled, nodded and finally came around to Nick.

''Shannon.'' He took her hand before she could yank it back. There was the briefest glance at the V in her dress.

''I understood you wouldn't touch this honor because it might blow your cover.''

''I'm flattered to be in this kind of company.''

''Instead of simply writing about it.''

''Ouch.''

''Karen Holland told me everything. No, I take that back. I don't suppose I'll ever know everything. Of course she had no inkling that I even knew you. Not that I do, you understand. Know you, that is.'' She wished she sounded less flustered.

"You made that clear last week at the picnic."

"What are you doing here?'' People were glancing at them and she lowered her voice to an angry whisper. "It doesn't make sense that you would guard your identity so religiously then pose for the cover of a magazine, unless of course I was the only one you wanted to confuse."

"I should have known you could misconstrue even this. I'm here because I knew you would be."

"I've swallowed enough. Don't ask me to believe that one."

"I'm not asking anything. The only one confused is me, Shannon. I've made a complete shambles of everything."

The stylist called them to gather around the ladder. Shannon tried to lower her voice even further. "I gave you every opportunity to explain, to come clean."

"For what? This kind of treatment? Risk never having you in my arms again?''

"Keep your voice down." They crossed the room.

"Then keep my hopes up," he replied as he left her and went back to the middle rung of the ladder.

His audacity kept her flushed and she glared as the photographer conferred with her two assistants. "Shannon—" Greta Mattson was signaling that she step forward as she framed a shot with her hands. "Sort of drape yourself back-to-back with Nick Hansen over there. Lean against each other. Nice contrast. Good height match.''

Before she could argue she was being poked and eased into position. ''Back,'' the photographer said. ''Both of you put your full weight against each other. Good. Perfect. Now a splash of red, Meredith Hartell, swirl the hem of your dress…''

Shannon stopped listening and tried to lighten the pressure as she pressed her bare shoulders against Nick's shirt. His draped jacket brushed her arm. She was tingling from head to toe and hating every minute of it.

''Same height, great balance. Sparks,'' Greta said to the stylist. She actually raised her eyebrows. ''I like that.''

Sparks. Daggers would have been a more appropriate description. For the rest of the session Shannon kept her mouth shut and let the professional manipulate her.

By the time they finished dusk had arrived. Across the river the real skyline glittered and looked as spectacular as the backdrop. The group dispersed and Nick caught up with her in the hall. ''With the possible exception of our Monday night, I've never seen you look more beautiful.''

She stopped. ''I'd like to forget *our* Monday night ever happened.''

He took her by the arm. ''Have you tried? All I've been able to do is remember.''

''You're a writer. There's no way I can compete

with all your clever remarks and constant innuendo. Now, if you'll excuse me, I was going to change and get out of here. You're supposed to pose with the other men.''

''You've done just fine in the innuendo department, Shannon, just fine in every department. I'm the one who's botched everything.''

''True.''

He traced the spaghetti strap on her shoulder. It did unseemly things to the rest of her. ''Don't change.'' He smoothed his cummerbund. ''Don't waste all this formal attire. Wait till I'm finished, then come with me. We have it on the best authority that we're two of the most eligible singles in Pittsburgh. Here we are dressed to the nines. There must be someplace we can go and impress the plebeians.''

''Maybe there's a wedding we could crash.''

''Humor. I'm encouraged. Let's go look for a prom we could sneak into.''

''Sorry, Nick, I'm on my way home. It's a Tuesday night and it's been a long day.''

''Dinner, then. Someplace really spiffy. You have to eat. Splurge with me, then I'll see you home safe and sound.''

''My car's in the lot. Coming within shouting distance of you isn't safe and I haven't been sound since that Sunday the rest of the city will soon read about.''

''I disguised you in the article.''

''Perky little blonde with anger worthy of a grizzly bear.''

''Have you read it?''

''No.'' She admitted that she only knew what Karen had told her.

''Wait for me and don't ask questions. I know just the place to discuss it.''

''I don't want to discuss it and it should be obvious to you by now that I hate surprises. Don't stand there giving me one of your studied looks like you can read my mind.''

''Lady, by now it should be obvious to you that reading your mind is a complete impossibility. I'm just asking you to trust me. I know I don't deserve it,'' he added as she opened her mouth. ''You complain that you don't know who I am. You've accused me of being a stranger. Give me another chance. Come with me and I'll share some things I love.''

''You still don't get it, do you, Nick? It's you I loved. That's all I wanted you to share. Not things— yourself.'' She pressed her open hand against the pleats of his dress shirt. ''Who you are, what you are, what you want to be. That's all I ever wanted from you.''

Genuine amazement softened his expression. ''You loved me? Let me earn it back—give you reason to love me again. I'll show you what makes my heart race and my blood run red. I'll share it all and I promise, hard as it will be, not to make a single pass.''

''Opening night at the opera? A fund-raiser at the Andy Warhol Museum? I can't think of what you love that we're dressed for.''

''I guess you'll have to trust me till we get there.

The rest of this photo session can't take too much longer. Will you wait for me?''

She held his troubled glance a moment longer than necessary. Love. They'd both thrown the word into the conversation without so much as a blink. She did love him. That was the hell of it. "I'll wait," she whispered.

The heat of the day had dissipated a little and dusk had deepened, although this late in June real darkness would hold off until after nine. Shannon watched the candles flicker in the still air. Nick had found a box of votive candles used to light the boathouse entrance during a fund-raiser for the Head of the Ohio regatta. Mallards honked as they nibbled at the shoreline for supper. Her dinner was in front of her.

They were on the balcony of the island boathouse at a table for two that Nick had pulled from the storage closet and draped with a disposable cloth. He served General Tso's chicken, stir-fried vegetables and fried rice on plastic plates and a very good California Chardonnay in throwaway tumblers. Dinnerware had come from the boathouse kitchen. The rest they'd picked up on Walnut Street on the way.

They were on the second floor, directly over the storage bays where the rowing shells, oars and launches were garaged. Her view was not of the river, but the narrow channel that separated the north side of the island from the mainland. Nick had also managed to confiscate the boom box from the workout room and classical music wafted above the hum of the city. The mallards squawked as an occasional rower or kayaker returned to the landing dock.

A second group of rowers, sweating in their workout clothes, glanced up at them on their way to store their gear. "You'd think they never seen a couple up here in formal clothes dining on Chinese takeout and listening to the Pittsburgh Symphony Orchestra."

"By candlelight," Shannon added.

Nick arched an eyebrow. "Humor. I like that in a woman."

She sighed. "The issue isn't what you like in a woman, Nick."

"Believe me, Green Eyes, I know what the issue is. My entire life is in flux."

"Not professionally."

The flicker of candles softened his features. "You're after truth, so here's a little more. You asked me why I agreed to the foolish magazine honor. Eighty percent was because I knew you'd be there."

"And the other twenty?"

"Midlife crisis." He laughed. "Not personal, professional. The article you're so steamed over, 'Borrowed Baby,' is written under my real name because I want to branch out. I'm thirty-one. It's time for credit for what I do, even when it's sardonic, and a little jaundiced. Being Jake O'Donnell is fun, amply pays the mortgage, but I'd like my readers to know I'm capable of more."

"So putting name to face isn't going to ruin you?"

His half smile melted her. "I was anonymous when I needed to be and look where that got me."

She made a point of glancing at the romantic setting. "You haven't done too shabbily."

"I don't want to be just 'Since You Asked' anymore. I've been at odds with Dan Miller, my editor at the paper, all year, which is why he was agreeable to my writing the article for Charlie Hutchinson at the magazine."

"You can't blame me for taking everything so personally. I'll admit I hadn't thought about your actions from a business standpoint or as career decisions. I just saw myself being used by fast-talking Jake O'Donnell."

"I used the events and circumstances when you reacted to Kip and me. For that I'm guilty as charged. The only other thing I'm guilty of is destroying this fledgling relationship while I was trying so hard not to screw it up."

She smiled. How could she not? "It's not destroyed, not entirely. Do you know what you want, Nick?"

He watched the channel and the ducks and got to his feet. "A dance with the most beautiful, intriguing woman who's ever come into my life."

"There's barely six feet of extra space out here," she said as she laughed.

"The less the better. I have a promise to keep and it's the only way I'm going to get you into my arms tonight."

She moved into his embrace. Nicholas Hansen had kept his promise and then some. The night was slipping by like the slow current in the channel and she'd seen more of the real Nick than in the weeks she'd known him. It wasn't the first time she'd fit perfectly into his arms, but it was the first time violins and cellos and the mood mellowing strains of French horns made it seem so perfect. She got lost in the moment as they moved slowly around the small space.

"Penny for your thoughts," he whispered.

"I was thinking that you're as talented vertical as you are horizontal." His laugh registered all the way down to the spot where his hand suddenly pressed against the base of her spine. They were falling into something comfortable and enticing and the memory of what they'd already shared kept her pulse quick and her cheeks warm. Before he could suggest what had to be as much on his mind as hers, she shifted. "I have a mountain of paperwork waiting for me at home, Nick, and a brutal day tomorrow. I'm sure you're due back over here at dawn again."

"The voice of reason." His tone was playful but he cupped the candles and blew them out without making a move to kiss her.

"Thank you for sharing this."

"I can get you copies of my dental records and college transcript if it would help. References on request, too."

Cleanup was barely more than stuffing garbage bags and wiping down the table and before she knew it they were walking from the now-dark boathouse out to their cars, the only ones in the lot. She wanted to tell him how handsome he looked under the moonlight all pensive and remorseful. Every hormone in her body was on alert. Greta Mattson had been right on the money about sparks.

He's going to ask. She could feel it between them like summer air heavy with static electricity, heat lightning. *And I'm going to stick to my resolve.*

''The best part of tonight has been hearing you laugh again, Shannon. Is a single kiss good-night too much to hope for?''

She raised her index finger. ''Maybe one.''

He put his hand under her hair, back there where the chords of her neck had been as tight as piano wire since her dinner with Karen. Her scalp tingled and heat raced to the arches of her feet. He kissed her. It was a kiss to melt the paint off a puppet. Her little black dress seemed to shrink as he opened his fingers and lifted the weight of her hair from her neck. The hollow of her throat burned. He was there, too, doing suggestive things with his other thumb just inside her crepe neckline. *He's going to ask and I'm going to turn him down.*

Love did this to people, made them reckless and aching to touch and stroke and whisper intoxicating things in the middle of deserted parking lots. He whispered in her ear and along her jaw and she had to keep her eyes open because closed all she saw was Nick Hansen in nothing but the pool of moonlight at her bedroom window.

Heat lightning. He will ask and I will turn him down. ''We forgot the fortune cookies,'' she whis-

pered before he reduced her to a puddle on the mac-
adam.

"I'd ask you to get them, but they're in my pocket,
Green Eyes. I've exhausted my self-control and
there's darn little left of yours." He laughed at her
soft gasp. "Can you see now that the fear that I might
ruin all this between us is what kept me lying. You're
the kind of woman Jake O'Donnell's never been able
to find, what any man aches for."

Maybe another night in his arms wouldn't hurt. He
loves you. Would those thick-lashed eyes lie after all
you've been through, after all you've shared, after all
this tonight?

"Half the reason I got myself into this mess, Shannon, is because I know what I've meant to you and I
was so damned afraid I'd lose it."

"I suppose it shows."

He was quiet. "You're incapable of a dishonest
emotion."

"That certainly puts me at a disadvantage."

"Advantage, disadvantage. Relationships aren't
tennis matches. Ironic, isn't it? I've built my whole
journalistic career around the premise that the battle
between the sexes is a constant, that men and women
are as much sparring partners as anything else."

"Do you believe it?"

"I did. Until very recently." His smile was rueful.
He pulled the wrapped fortune cookies from his
pocket and handed it to her.

"I'll read mine later." She had to clear her throat
to get the words out.

"Good idea." He pocketed his and kept the summer air between them. "Shannon, for once my timing is perfect."

Here it comes, she thought, still unsure of whether she'd say yes or no and how to explain her need for time away from him.

"I needed to see you tonight because I'm leaving tomorrow. I'll be out at our family place at High Pines for the Fourth of July, then I head for a rowing camp I support for high-risk kids who need a healthy outlet. It's an annual thing I do every July. Some coaching, advising...role model stuff. I'll be out of town most of the month. I'm sure you'll agree that under the circumstances, I think it'll do us both some good."

Time apart...a month...both some good. That's what she'd meant to say. After kissing her into X-rated fantasies he was stealing her lines, her thunder, the rug from under her feet. She had to clear her throat again to get her voice to hold, but she swallowed her shock and nodded. "I was about to suggest the same thing. The rest of the month might not even be enough."

"Good. Then we agree." His smile implied that her actions might have suggested otherwise. Without so much as another kiss, he led her to her car.

By the time she remembered the fortune cookie, she was home, propped in bed by herself listening to the hum of the air-conditioning and channel surfing with the television remote. She fished it out of her purse and opened it under the lamp beside her bed. *Soon your heart will speak its own language.* Her heart had been speaking its own language for three pulse-pounding, ego-shredding weeks. "It's Greek to me, already," she muttered and turned off the light.

She celebrated the July Fourth holiday at Lake Scituate with her brothers and extended family. She'd been sworn to secrecy about the upcoming magazine issue. She put Nick Hansen in the same category and stayed tight-lipped about him as well, even after she sat on the porch and read his column. "Since You Asked" was about baseball that week. It was funny, nonconfrontational and inoffensive. Downright bland, now that she knew how much heat the author could generate. The temptation to spill everything, from the magazine to the true identity of Jake O'Donnell, drove her back to Thurston Court. The last thing she wanted was any older-brother advice on the ways and wiles of men.

Pittsburgh was in its usual celebratory summer mood: fireworks after the Pirates games, boating regattas at the Point, antique car rallies in Schenley Park, Sunday brunch concerts on the grounds of the Center for the Arts. She took them all in with friends, lots of friends, new ones, business associates, neighbors, anything to keep her mind occupied.

Nick Hansen was out of her hair exactly as she'd planned. All right, he was gone because it was exactly what he'd planned. The results were the same. She had lots of time to think. She rattled around in her air-conditioned condominium, she rattled around in her shop and analyzed her situation to death. Was it the Chinese who cautioned to be careful what you wished for, it might just come true?

Kip and Kate Goulding paid her a surprise visit to the shop. Kip's mother looked like her pictures and now that they were face-to-face, Shannon could see the resemblance to Nick. It seemed years ago that she'd thought Kate Goulding was an ex-wife. Kip had Kisses in one arm and Whiffle, the puppet she'd given him, on his hand.

"I understand you've been very generous to Nicholas. To Kip." She laughed. "I'm trying to remember the nickname."

"It's a cute one."

"Another of my brother's bright ideas." She didn't offer any more explanation.

Shannon ached to discuss Nick Hansen's bright idea. She couldn't. She wanted to ask if Kate had heard from him, but that would imply that she knew he was away. Kate might ask when she'd seen him last and that had been for the secret photo shoot. It strained the conversation.

Kate stayed charming and noncommittal. It was impossible to tell how much she knew, or didn't know, about what her brother had been up to, or even if she guessed that Shannon might already be familiar with the layout of her town house. They finished with small talk and a promise to visit each other on Thurston Court.

A two-week children's puppet making workshop filled the heart of the month. By then she'd given up expecting a postcard. When the man said incommunicado he meant it.

On Friday Shannon got around to reading the newspaper during a break at work. She opened the *Register* to the latest "Since You Asked" column over coffee and yogurt in her shop studio. Top Ten Criteria For Making My Most Eligible List had been set in bold print right under the cigar-chomping photo. "What the heck is he up to?" she muttered.

"Who?" Meg Bazley was asking as she unpacked a shipment of miniature print dollhouse wallpapers.

Shannon cleared her thoughts. "Jake O'Donnell's got some trumped-up list for his own most eligible list."

"A tie-in to the *Three Rivers Magazine* issue coming out next month, I bet. Let me guess. He wants a woman who never touches the remote control, knows the Stanley Cup, World Series, Super Bowl winners since 1960, knows how to get spaghetti sauce out of neckties and makes cakes from scratch."

Shannon laughed as she glanced at Meg, aware that a month ago she would have scoffed at the title and read no further. "You're not far off, but for once I think he's joking."

"You think so?"

"Maybe. He was here, you know."

"Jake O'Donnell in here? Buying something for a grandchild?"

Shannon shook her head. "The guy behind the column is Nick Hansen. He was here with his nephew,

Kip Goulding. The little boy I tested the Scarvelli puppets on.''

"Wait a minute. That gorgeous guy you kissed over there by the door?''

Shannon raised an eyebrow. "You never said anything.''

"You're the one who's never said anything." Meg laughed. "I figured if you wanted me to know, you'd mention it.''

"You're right.''

Meg gathered the small rolls of wallpaper into her hands. "That's all the information I get after keeping quiet all these weeks?''

"Sorry. There's nothing to tell. We dated a few times, that's all." She went back to the paper as Meg left the room. At the bottom of the column Nick waxed poetic about the real criteria the magazine used: social conscience, community activism, charm, grace, the power to affect change or at least to effect people, a commitment to the city. It was flattering to think that her volunteer efforts and the offerings of her shop put her in such vaulted company. What tugged at her heart was that Nicholas Hansen had met that criteria, too; a Nicholas Hansen still unknown to her.

Wednesday a small courier-delivered package was waiting when she returned to Time Out from lunch. Inside was a broken fortune cookie and its telltale slip of paper. *Your words are your fortune. Invest wisely.* Nick's from their dinner at the boathouse? Message meant for me? Meant for Nick? Meant for me to know it had been meant for Nick? The courier office was farther down Fifth Avenue in Oakland. Nick was home. Or had he made the arrangements before he left through Kate or Karen Holland or one of his cronies she hadn't met. She didn't know much but she was sure that trying to investigate would only lead her down a dozen blind alleys. Maybe that's what Nick was waiting for. She sighed and then she laughed. For once she was enjoying the intrigue.

Busywork and determination got Shannon to the final week in July. Tuesday afternoon Evan called and insisted she use the cottage since the rest of the family had plans and obligations. She agreed. She needed to get out of town.

"Key's over the door on the porch."

"I know."

"Remember to switch the pilot light back to full setting on the hot water tank."

"And check the mailbox. I know the routine."

"I know, but I thought you could use some reminders. You've seemed a little distracted this month when you've been up there with us."

"A lot on my mind."

"Who?"

"Not who," she lied. "Work." He didn't give her any argument.

Friday morning, completely out of character, she opened the *Register* to "Since You Asked" before reading any other part of the paper. In fact the editorial section blew off the patio table as she folded back the page she was after. Jake O'Donnell still chomped his cigar, still wore that smirk. It's A Gut Thing was the headline.

Advantage, Miss Gleam - in - her - eye. Advantage, Mr. O'Donnell. Tennis? Guess again. We're talking Battle of the Sexes, sparring worthy of any contender inside the ropes. That's the way the game is played, or so I thought.

So I thought. Shannon skimmed the column then went back to the top and started again. Nick Hansen had written about love. All right, he called it "the *L* word" and referred to it as a four-letter utterance that could stop a guy in his tracks faster than any profanity.

Ironic. I've built my journalistic career around the premise that men and women are at opposite poles, that the Battle of the Sexes is a constant...

Jake O'Donnell, in his inimitable style, was confessing to falling in love. "With me," she whispered to the empty patio. She read the column a third time. It was a paraphrase of his soliloquy in the parking lot the last time she'd seen him. "Nick Hansen—" She laughed and sighed and leaned back in her chair. She didn't know where he was or how to reach him. He knew darn well he was reaching her. This wasn't fair, but it sure felt good.

By closing time that afternoon she was more than ready to get out of town. She'd armed herself with

house magazines and catalogs of dollhouse parts to
fill the empty hours. She intended to swim and read
and clear her head and then she intended to plot. August was just days away. Nick couldn't stay away
forever. When he returned she would be ready to get
him at his own game. She just had to figure out how.

It was dark by the time she pulled off the main
road and stopped at the mailbox that signaled the
McEvoy lakeside property. Sticking her hand in the
darkened box usually brought nothing but spiders or
a week's worth of ads. Tonight, flyers and junk mail.
She snapped on the overhead light in the car for a
closer look so she could discard it all in the waste bin
before she unlocked the cottage. Tucked under the
free newspaper and advertising leaflets for the local
mall's furniture clearance was a manila envelope.

Fear was unwarranted, but a sliver of concern gave
her chills. There was no return address and no post-
mark, but it was addressed to her with the correct
rural delivery box number. She ran her thumb under
the flap and tore it open. She gasped and laughed and
talked to herself as she slid out a photocopy of a
typeset article. ''Borrowed Baby or How I Tried to
Make Myself Irresistible to Women'' by Nick Hansen
sat on top of a full-color, eight-by-ten glossy print of
the cover of the September issue of *Three Rivers
Magazine*. This time she laughed out loud.

Nick was at the top of the ladder leaning against
her, just the way Greta Mattson had posed them. The
remaining men and women fanned out around them
in a pyramid. Nick, however, had been circled in

black marker. TAKE ME OUT OF CIRCULATION was printed in block letters across the top. She had to wipe her eyes with the back of her arm as she turned the car onto the hard-pack gravel lane that meandered along the shoreline to the family cottage. She was confused and elated and in the middle of nowhere, emotionally as well as physically, until the man with all the right words got himself back on his island and back into her arms.

Fifty yards from the cottage she realized lights glowed through the gauzy screens of her wide front porch. At ten yards her headlights caught the shadow of a familiar Jeep parked nearly in the woods next to the toolshed.

Shannon left everything in the car and crossed the pine-needled ground with her heart slamming against her ribs. Nick Hansen was sitting in the wicker rocker with a book open in his lap and a mug on the table next to the lamp as if he owned the place. She wanted the first words, something witty and profound and casual.

"Nicholas Goulding Hansen O'Donnell—" was all she could say.

He grinned and got to his feet. "I'll answer to any of them."

"Answers. You better have a few more."

"You, too, Green Eyes. Do you really think it's appropriate for a man of my journalistic stature and reputation to be called Geranium Man by your brother?"

"You and Evan hatched this?"

"First I had to convince him that my intentions were honorable. Seems he thought I was married and lived on Thurston Court with my family. Then I had to convince him that I needed a secluded place without puppets and two-year-olds and fax machines and anxious editors in which to propose. Evan wanted to know exactly what it was I intended to propose. The guy wants as many answers as you do."

"We McEvoys stick together." By the time she got that reply out, Nick had her in his arms. She sighed against him as if she'd held her breath for the four long weeks he'd been gone. "What do you intend to propose, Nick?"

He pulled a fortune cookie out of his pocket and handed it to her. She moved closer to the lamplight and snapped it open. An ornate silver band set with a diamond and sapphires fell into her palm.

"It was my grandmother's."

"How on earth?"

Nick put his arm around her again and led her off the porch and into the dark cottage. "Shannon McEvoy, you'll have to marry me to get that answer."

"Nicholas Hansen, you have the whole weekend to convince me that I should."

* * * * *

Look for a new and exciting series from Harlequin!

HARLEQUIN

Duets™

Two __new__ full-length novels in one book, from some of your favorite authors!

Starting in May, each month we'll be bringing you two new books, each book containing two brand-new stories about the lighter side of love! Double the pleasure, double the romance, for less than the cost of two regular romance titles!

Look for these two new Harlequin Duets™ titles in May 1999:

Book 1:
WITH A STETSON AND A SMILE
by Vicki Lewis Thompson
THE BRIDESMAID'S BET
by Christie Ridgway

Book 2:
KIDNAPPED? by Jacqueline Diamond
I GOT YOU, BABE by Bonnie Tucker

2 GREAT STORIES BY 2 GREAT AUTHORS FOR 1 LOW PRICE!

Don't miss it! Available May 1999 at your favorite retail outlet.

HARLEQUIN®
Makes any time special.™

Look us up on-line at: http://www.romance.net   HDGENR

Looking For More Romance?

Visit Romance.net

Check in daily for these and other exciting features:

Hot off the press

View all current titles, and purchase them on-line.

What do the stars have in store for you?

Horoscope

Hot deals

Exclusive offers available only at Romance.net

Plus, don't miss our interactive quizzes, contests and bonus gifts.

PWEB

This March Silhouette is proud to present

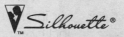

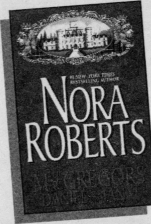

FORTUNE'S Children™

*The Fortune family requests
the honor of your presence at the weddings of*

FORTUNE'S CHILDREN™

The Brides

Silhouette Desire's scintillating new miniseries,
featuring the beloved Fortune family
and five of your favorite authors.

***The Honor Bound Groom*—January 1999**
by Jennifer Greene (SD #1190)

***Society Bride*—February 1999**
by Elizabeth Bevarly (SD #1196)

And look for more **FORTUNE'S CHILDREN:
THE BRIDES** installments by Leanne Banks,
Susan Crosby and Merline Lovelace,
coming in spring 1999.

Available at your favorite retail outlet.

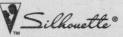

Silhouette®